"Imagination is the most marvelous, miraculous, inconceivably powerful force the world has ever known."

- Napoleon Hill

Map of Helsyndel created by Nathan T. Challis
Map illustrations by cartographybird

Table of Contents

I - Moonlit Shadows

II - Heralds of War

III - Aethelred

IV - Tsura

V - Iceclaw Cave

VI - Bone Island

VII - The Realm of Obscurity

VIII - The Bearer of Darkness

IX - Babbling Brook

X - Umeko

XI - Crooks Hollow

XII - The Banneret Vanguard

XIII - The Siren

XIV - Aliyah

XV - The Reaper

XVI - Balmelech

XVII - Kraken Moon

XVIII - Illusions of Gold

XIX - Saeculum Secunda

XX - The Halls of Amenti

Continents of Helsyndel

Illthashore: What a magnificent place Illthashore is! There is no other continent with as many diverse beings, peculiar customs and creative arts. Those who live there are blessed by the Gods to live in a place of such beauty and magic. The Arcaneus, a powerful conclave of wizards and magic practitioners, can be found to the east of Trisail Lake, upon the shores of which sits Illthashore's gleaming capital— Ellicade. Emperor Herman Troil resides in Ellicade, presiding over his lands with a firm but benevolent hand. Darkness, however, has always been a part of Illthashore's vibrant history. Virulent evils have walked the lands, leaving a stain on Illthashore for generations to come.

"Illthashore is an extraordinary place, but so too is it dark and dangerous. Tread not off the woodland paths, for the wilds are home to more than just wolves and bears."

— Emperor Herman Troil

Alland: It would be a difficult task to find a land as serenely unique as that of the noble continent of Alland. The vast, rolling plains of the western regions bow to the awesome majesty of the eastern mountain ranges. It is nestled within the north-most of these mountains that Alland's capital, Gispia, can be found. Ruled by King Pelin Adalhart and the royal family, Gispia has long been a beacon of civility for the citizens of Alland. Separated from Gispia by Royalwave Lake, to the south, is the smaller city of Newhelm. Newhelm houses the Order of the Golden Eagle, a faction of knights who uphold the law and maintain peace throughout the land. The knights must also hold at bay the goblin-kin hordes who call the eastern mountains home, and who regularly attempt sieges on Gispia and its neighboring villages.

"I wouldn't have chosen anywhere else to grow up. Alland has been my home since I was born, and I love everything about it. The people, the land, the wildlife. The majesty of the mountains, the tranquility of the endless plains to the west, the wonder of its forests. I love it all."

— Taya Adalhart, daughter of King Pelin and Queen
Melenna Adalhart

Stethe: Stethe is not for the faint of heart or those with weak constitution. In ancient times the land erupted with plumes of lava that arched for the skies. Volcanic mountains rose from the ground and molten fissures formed into rivers of fire. The land became slag; nothing grew. Still, humans came to settle from the east. The city of Krona, Stethe's capital, was born of human ingenuity and the sheer power of will. Nobody knows what Stethe was really like before it became scorched by fire, only murals from an antediluvian age give evidence of a once luscious and bountiful jungle that blanketed the continent. Jocelyn Scorne, the officially appointed protectorate of Stethe, presides over her people from Krona, always ready to battle the hordes of outlying vagabonds and bandits that threaten their way of life.

"Double the watch outside and inside the city. I want any suspicious activity within our walls reported immediately. We will not be caught off guard when the attack comes."

— Jocelyn Scorne, responding to intelligence of an impending bandit raid on Krona

Viridian Isles: Central to Helsyndel is the Viridian Isles, home to a hardy people who have always governed themselves. The rolling green pastures of this small continent have been considered to be one of the most peaceful places in Helsyndel. The troubles of the world seem distant to Viridish people, it is rare indeed that evil would visit their doorstep — and if it did it would quickly get a Viridish boot in its rear! Academics and philosophers from abroad have often used the Viridian Isles as a place to escape the bustling world. Here they come to think, to ponder, and to be at peace when life weighs heavily upon them. Argishill serves as the capital of the Isles. The thatched-roofed homes of the village have stood strong through the tests of time, as has the community that calls this place home.

"If there is a place where true peace can be found, it is here on the Viridian Isles. The people here want for nothing. They live contentedly as they are without outside influence, foreign commerce, or the grievances of politics."

— Lexie Marcelina, Knight of the Order the Golden Eagle

Wellhaven: Portshield, the capital of Wellhaven, is also known as the Den of Thieves. The small continent has always been known for its devious and dishonest denizens. Pirates, thieves, blades for hire, smugglers, and other unscrupulous tricksters fill the taverns of Wellhaven night after night. Though technically part of Illthashore and owned by the Emperor, Wellhaven has always held, at best, only a loosely acknowledged affiliation with its larger brethren continent. Duke Kean Witherborn presides over Wellhaven, as appointed by the emperor. The Imperial fort on the southern shores has always been maintained as a reminder of where Wellhaven's allegiances truly lie, but, even so, the scoundrels of Portshield have always lived however they so desire.

"I like it here in Wellhaven. I belong here, amongst the thieves and cutthroats. It's easy to evade the law and — if you're good at what you do — there are no repercussions. I could get used to this."

— Yuliya Tatiana, blade for hire

Gelid Island: Perhaps the least inhabited landmass in all of Helsyndel, the Gelid Islands' only settlement is Baffilin. Lost souls and social castaways reside here. Those who venture to Baffilin do so because they have nowhere else to go. The frostbitten wilds outside of Baffilin are utterly inhospitable but to the most stalwart survivors or those possessed of an otherworldly nature. Necromancers, sorcerers, and other practitioners of dark magic also frequent the islands. The solitude allows them to practice their sinister arts in peace and far from the law. The hand of the empire does not extend to the Gelid Islands. It has always been, and will always be, a cold and destitute place.

"The Gelid Islands? Better to steer clear. Even if we don't run into trouble ashore I can guarantee we will have stow-aways when we set sail again. Not typical stow-aways either. I mean the dangerous kind. The sort that will murder us in the night and reanimate our corpses to sail the ship in our stead."

— Axton Hartwell, Captain of the HMIS Avatar — a fully rigged First Rate Ship of the Line in service of the Imperial Navy

Neverthaw: Neverthaw, like Stethe, is a nearly inhospitable place. Violent blizzards whipping down from the northern mountain ranges are a common occurrence for the people of Chillhorn—Neverthaw's capital—and its neighboring villages. Despite the land's arctic ferocity, however, life has always flourished on Neverthaw. Nomad settlements dot the continent and many unique factions have always called the snowy tundra home. Yeti, wuhlfs, and behrs are creatures that can only be found on Neverthaw. King Bjørn Valdemar rules Neverthaw from Aldrithaw, his towering castle in the heart of Neverthaw's wilds.

"In the known history of Neverthaw, no foreign army has ever come to its shores with the intent to wage war. Neverthaw is just too harsh and unwelcoming for those not born and raised in this land. The people of Neverthaw possess a strength and courage not known to most others."

— Aloysias Silas, Abbott of Whiteflame Abbey

Udjata: Hot and dry are the two best words to describe the southern continent of Udjata. The desert land, like Illthashore, has a history steeped in darkness and the occult. Ranoub Nefer, Udjata's sovereign ruler, must regularly send patrols into the desert to drive back the sepulchral beings that threaten his domain. Udjata's capital, Asera, located on the northwestern tip of the continent, is a hub for trade and commerce. Asera is considered the only truly safe place in Udjata, largely due to its umbrella of protection from the Udjatan military. Even so, the Great Sands of Udjata are considered one of the most stunning sights in Helsydel.

"An assassin of Aukeket does not need your money. They will take it, but the thrill of the hunt and its grisly conclusion is payment enough."

— Kamenwati, High Priest of Apeptsut, speaking of an elite sect of Udjatan assassins

Ocoya: Far across the seas of the known world there lies a continent that was until recently unknown to Helsyndilians. Contact with the people of this continent, Ocoyans, has been sporadic at best. Messengers from both sides have been sent across the sea to establish diplomatic relations, but only little progress has been made as of yet. The Ocoyans are very withdrawn, it seems as if they only communicate with Illthashore because they feel politically obligated to do so. They seem indifferent to having discovered a new civilization. Relations aside, their sovereign, Emperor Nakayama Meiji, rules over a most beautiful land. The Ocoyan capital, Heodo, is nestled amidst a treacherous mountain range. The only way to get to the regal city of Heodo is to ascend the innumerable stone steps up the side of the mountain to the heavily guarded city gates at the top. Watchtowers dot the stairs leading up to the city, which seems nigh impregnable. Ocoya has become known for its incredibly disciplined regime and the unyielding warriors who call it home.

"Ocoyan's are a fiercely assiduous people, their whole lives are spent in pursuit of self-mastery and perfection. Though not much is yet known about their ways, there is no doubt that angering them would be most unwise."

- Marcus Valens, explorer

Known Races of Helsyndel

Human - native to all of Helsyndel, humans are the dominant race in the world. The largest population of humans can be found on Illthashore.

Aroz - a race of merfolk found in the Iceing Sea. They regularly trade with shoreline human settlements and are frequently contracted to protect HMIS ships.

Shifters - a cunning race of beings from Stethe who have adopted a natural camouflage as their greatest asset. They are often mercenaries and assassins.

Yeti - brutish humanoids that call Neverthaw home. Yeti's do not deal with the civilized races in any capacity and are feared across Neverthaw.

Spriggan - beings that live in total harmony with nature and have themselves become plantlike. They live on an island off the north-east coast of Illthashore.

Goblins - small, aggressive humanoids that can be found predominantly on Alland, but also on Illthashore and Naverthaw. Goblins are often hostile to any not of their ilk and are constantly at war with the knights of Gispia and Newhelm.

Terram - an ancient race of subterranean humans who have evolved to adapt to the lightless silence of their vast underground network of caves, tunnels and subterrestrial cities.

Demons - Demons come from the Void. Long ago a portal was opened that allowed them to leak into Helsyndel from their own plane of existence. Demons are malignant creatures that take great pleasure in causing pain and misery.

Vampires - any race except the spriggan and demons can be infected with the disease called Vampari Hemonecro. When any other species becomes infected they will become what is known as a Blood Hunter, a being of the night that consumes the blood of its victims and thrives on the hunt.

The Imperial Legion and the Empire

Emperor Herman Troil rules over Illthashore, and in turn nearly all of Helsyndel. There are many orders and factions sanctioned under his name, such as the Banneret Vanguard, the Shadow Seekers, the Discipuli, and the lesser known Tacitum Obscurum. Herman was bequeathed his title of Emperor by the Helsyn Family, of whom very little is known. The Empire is overshadowed and maintained by the Emperor's Imperial Legion. The Legion, as well as being a massive army to bring to bear, is primarily a peace keeping force throughout Helsyndel.

Ranks of the Imperial Legion

Grand High Constable - overseer of the Imperial Legion.

Regional High Constable - oversees the Legion in their region.

Marshal/Field Marshal - in command of a regiment.

General - commands a battalion.

Captain - high ranking officer, highest rank in a Legion fort.

Commander - commands a company.

Upper Class Legionnaire - commands a platoon.

Lower Class Legionnaire - commands a squadron.

Swordsman/Agent - trainer of recruits/spy (infiltrator).

Soldier/Archer - footsoldiers under the command of higher ranking individuals.

Spearman - the first line of defense in the field.

Recruit - one who is in training.

Serf - cares for a Legion fort/camps/cooks.

↳Imperial Naval Ships

HMIS Courageous (Captain Amelia Gail)

Brigantine, 12 Guns
Service of the Imperial Navy
98 Souls
Square Rigged Sails

HMIS Hero (Captain Odo)

Warship, 58 Guns
Service of the Imperial Navy
332 Souls
Three Masts

HMIS Champion (Captain Eldon Wade)

Warship, 62 Guns
Service of the Imperial Navy
350 Souls
Three Masts
3rd Rate

HMIS Vengeance (Captain Emmerson)

Warship, 68 Guns
Service of the Imperial Navy
365 Souls
Three Masts
3rd Rate

HMIS Haste (Captain Jak Fortune)

Schooner, 8 Guns
Service of the Imperial Navy
66 Souls
Two Masts

HMIS Avatar (Captain Axton Hartwell)

First Rate Ship of the Line, 100 Guns
Service of the Imperial Navy
789 Souls
Fully Rigged

HMIS Excursion (Captain Flint)

Merchant Ship, 14 Guns
Service of the Imperial Navy
53 Souls
Three Masts

HMIS Buoyant (Captain Edaline Beryl)

Galleon, 24 Guns
Service of the Imperial Navy
99 Souls
Fully Rigged

HMIS Stalwart (Captain Caldwell Daker)

Warship, 64 Guns
Service of the Imperial Navy
358 Souls
Three Masts
3rd Rate

HMIS Adept (Captain Acton Landers)

Frigate, 38 Guns
Service of the Imperial Navy
204 Souls
Fully Rigged

HMIS Duchess (Captain Hallan Rainer)

Frigate, 38 Guns
Service of the Imperial Navy
200 Souls
Fully Rigged

HMIS Deity (Captain Kemp Kelton)

First Rate Ship of the Line, 114 Guns
Service of the Imperial Navy
812 Souls
Fully Rigged

HMIS Hope (Captain Jagger Norwood)

Brigantine, 14 Guns
Service of the Imperial Navy
107 Souls
Square Rigged Sails

HMIS Ethereal (Captain Sherman)

Schooner, 10 Guns
Service of the Imperial Navy
70 Souls
Two Masts

HMIS Rival (Captain Maddox)

Warship, 74 Guns
Service of the Imperial Navy
381 Souls
Three Masts
3rd Rate

The Fifteen Ships of His Magesty's Imperial Navy

The Gispian Monarchy

The Gispian Royal Family rules over Alland just as Emperor Herman Troil rules over Illthashore. However, while Herman's influence stretches to almost every corner of Helsyndel, the emperor's hand has never held sway over events in Alland. Relations between the neighboring continents have never been in question, but King Pelin Adalhart and Queen Melena Adalhart have always insisted on the sole sovereignty of their own nation.

Much of Alland's commerce comes from the sea, particularly from the Aroz. The merfolk and the Royal Family have always had excellent relations. Sorsegg Mal "the Tidebender", proclaimed Lord of the Iceing Sea and King of the Aroz, has always held Allandians in high regard and will send Aroz warriors to defend their ships in return for goods from the surface.

King Pelin Adalhart has always made certain that Alland maintains its stately repute throughout Helsyndel.

Deities of Helsyndel

Udjatan Pantheon - the hierarchy of divine beings that rule over the continent of Udjata. The sovereign of Udjata—Ranoub Nefer—is the only one who may be permitted by the high priests to communicate directly with the pantheon. The people of Udjata pray to the Udjatan gods at the exclusion of all others.

The Creator
Kher - god of all creation, sun and moon.

The Storm God
Asifeh - god of the skies, weather and wind.

The Earth Goddess
Tebeh - goddess of the land, stone and soil.

The Brine God
Muhati - god of the sea, tides and currents.

The Inferno God
Jalhab - god of fire, heat and desiccation.

Goddess of Harmony

Anensi - goddess of the elements, order and law.

Goddess of Change

Akhtera - goddess of innovation, progress and invention.

God of Battle

Saif - god of war, combat and victory.

Goddess of Vitality

Tabiah - goddess of nature, animals and plants.

The Duplicitous God

Mashaxah - god of deceit, trickery and mischief.

The Goddess of Being

Akhmot - goddess of life, women and birth.

The God of Mortality

Sef - god of death, afterlife and decay.

God of Judgment

Hahkmetzen - god of intellect, wisdom and reasoning.

Avaeos, the Lightning Phoenix - known as the patriarch of Helsyndel. It is said that it was he who molded the earth and shaped the skies. He and his daughter, Celestia, possess shrines on the Isle of Divinity. Avaeos is locked in an eternal power struggle with his brother, Madreas, who is a powerful Deadraiser and the apotheosis of evil.

Celestia - daughter of Avaeos. She presides over the heavens and is said to maintain the lunar cycle. The Maidens of Celestia, as well as the Crusaders of Avaeos, are the first line of defense against the otherworldly evils that plague Helsyndel.

Madreas, Origin of Darkness - brother of Avaeos, who imprisoned him in the Void, Madreas has enslaved an army of bloodthirsty demons and other aberrations during his time in isolation from Helsyndel. Madreas vies to bring darkness to the world and murder Avaeos for imprisoning him. He proclaimed himself as the first Deadraiser, blending dark sorcery and necromancy to wreak havoc on all who oppose him.

Alzehmov the Charnel Lord - the deity of the afterlife in Helsyndel. He is often worshiped by necromancers, assassins, and soldiers who frequent the field of battle. The Charnel Lord possesses a shrine on Solus Island, right next to Fort Vigilance on the Iceing Sea.

Mal'ethiel, Matriarch of the Arcane Arts - Mal'ethiel brought magic to the world of Helsyndel. From time to time she will inhabit the body of a mortal woman in order to walk the physical plain. She did so often during the Arcane War and the Riverine War. Her shrine is south-east of Soul Lake, north of the Arcaneus.

Murdagh, the Fiendish - while not a true divine being, he is still worshiped as one by thieves, rogues, bandits, and sometimes assassins. It is speculated that Murdagh was born in Portshield, to unknown parents, and now resides either somewhere in the Hills of Argus on the Viridian Isles or underground below Baffilin on Gelid Island.

Cyrqyx, Father of the Deep - lord of the waters, Cyrqyx is often worshiped by the Aroz, sailors, pirates, and coastal villages. He commands the waves, the tides, and the storms that sweep the high seas. The shrine of Cyrqyx can be located on the Gelid Islands, south of Baffilin.

Firn, Mistress of the North Wind - all northerners know and worship the goddess Firn. Her shrine is located on a derelict island just off the north-west coast of Neverthaw. Many have perished making the pilgrimage to her shrine, succumbing to the terrible frigid winds of the north. It is said that harsh blizzards sweep down from the mountains when her mood is foul.

Stories
of
Helsyndel

Moonlit Shadows

Bare feet padded quickly up the stone steps to the heavy chapel door. Moonlight shone down between the clouds, casting long, eerie shadows along the grounds. It was the sort of night that bore an unearthly chill, when ominous winds blew, and gossamer whispers dwelt just beyond the veil of perception.

Marritha scrabbled at the door, sobbing, dressed only in a delicate white nightgown. Her hair was a disheveled mess and her legs trembled with fear, threatening to give out.

At last she turned the knob, swung the door open, and all but fell into the chapel. She spun to shut the door, positive that the specters which woke her and chased her into the night were close on her heels.

Inside the chapel was warm and inviting. Lambent light issued from many candles along the walls and at the altar ahead, where the chapel's priest stood aghast. The pews were not occupied by many, but those that were in prayer turned to regard her. Their eyes did not linger; they seemed annoyed by the intrusion.

Marritha sniffed, calming her racing heart and drying her tears on her sleeve. She walked towards the altar, beginning to feel the night's chill leave her flesh.

"I'm sorry for the interruption," she whispered to the priest, who was the only one in the chapel still regarding her. She kept her eyes to the floor.

"My child," he began, stepping out from behind the altar, clearly unsure what to do next. He was an older man with kind features and greying hair. "You need to leave here."

Marritha glanced up, furrowing her brow.

"I...I can't," she stammered. "There are-"

The priest shook his head but made no move towards her. "Do you know what time it is?"

The numbness of fear washed over her as her heart began beating faster again. She hadn't stopped to consider it, until now. The hour was late, that was certain, and no church service would be conducted in the dead of night.

She looked to the pew's occupants, whose heads were bowed but for one man. His eyes bore into her, unblinking and with an air of obvious contempt. Beside him knelt his wife, who held her head low over clasped hands. Marritha watched as the woman lifted her gaze, enough so that she could glimpse her face beneath the bonnet she wore, and saw the woman's eyes roll up to affix her with pallid white pupils. Marritha spun away with a quiet squeak and glanced back up at the priest.

"This is not a place for the living," he said, "not at this hour. Please, go."

Marritha nodded, trembling, and turned towards the door. The woman in the bonnet stood there, behind her, barring her way. Her knees grew weak as the woman's gaunt face grew dark and her lower jaw unhinged and stretched. Marritha was accosted by a keening, banshee-like wail that overwhelmed her senses. She screamed, fell to the floor cowering, and shuffled back against the head pew with her hands held tight over her ears. She stayed there with her eyes screwed shut, rocking back and forth, expecting the end.

When death didn't come, she hesitantly opened her eyes. The chapel was empty, the candles dark, and the light of the moon her only blessing.

Fear rooted her to the spot. The ghastly occupants of the chapel might have gone, but she felt as if she was still not alone. Ice crept into her limbs. Ever so slowly she leaned over to look past the arm of the pew bench. There, in the deep shadows by the chapel door, where the pews were being swallowed by an inky void, were two pinpricks of light—eyes that pierced her very soul.

She clasped her hand over her mouth to stifle a gasp. The creature the eyes belonged to moved into the moonlight filtering through the windows. Its mangy hide clung to it like a patchwork carpet haphazardly tossed over a saddle rail, revealing a sickening amalgamation of flesh and bone beneath.

Four wicked antlers sprouted from its skull, where the jaw of its cervine skull showed through shorn flesh. The creature bellowed, spraying spittle and droplets of blood on the floor.

Would that it had not already seen her, but she knew it had. It leveled its deathly gaze at her, antlers lowered for the killing blow. Marritha stood, ready to run—although to where she wasn't sure—when the creature bellowed again. This time it released a pulse of dark energy that swept over her, sending her spinning into the altar and crumpling to the steps below.

Darkness took her, but before it did she saw the creature, this apex of death, stalking in for the kill.

*****

From the rafters above she saw the creature even before the woman on the ground did. She watched their interaction below with interest, and then, at the last second before the woman in the nightgown would have been impaled on those antlers, she swooped down to intercept the beast.

The creature reared up defensively, kicking at her and grunting in surprise. It did retreat however, not wishing to contend with the one who interrupted its next meal.

The woman's savior spread her wings and rose from the crouch she landed in. Silver, scintillating armor adorned her body and golden hair cascaded over her shoulders.

"I will not abide you in this place, demon of old. Take your nightmares and go."

The creature cocked its head curiously but seemed unwilling to make a move against her.

"I will purge you and your ilk from Helsyndel," she promised, "you have no place in this world."

It stamped the floor, seeming frustrated and angry. Then, it burst open the door and sprinted into the night. She heard the clacking of its hooves on stone receding into the distance and let go the breath she'd been holding. Despite her innate protection against beasts of nightmare, she would not have chosen to tangle with this one tonight.

She glanced down at the poor young woman on the floor, with her wild hair and dried tears. Terror had visited her, and only by the grace of good fortune would she wake to see the sunrise.

Without another look back she left the chapel, knowing that, for the rest of the night at least, no demon or slinking horror would intrude upon it.

It was time to commence the hunt.

Heralds of War

The night was like any other night on the Iceing Sea. Calm, quiet, and crisp.

At least it was until one of the riggers spotted flashes of light in the distant fog.

The captain, Edaline Beryl of Litus, was immediately roused from her slumber. She clambered up from below deck with two nervous deckhands in tow. I knew when I saw her expression turn to one of evident fear that we probably wouldn't survive the night.

"Douse the lights!" she hissed. "Now!"

I and the many other sailors aboard rushed to do just that. We stood at the rails after the deck was plunged into darkness, watching the flashes of red and gold illuminate the roiling fog from within. Every so often I could see silhouettes of winged beings. There were multiple combatants, some with large, supple wings and others with sharp, angular wings.

The lot of us had sailed with Edaline on the HMIS Bouyant, a fully rigged galleon in the service of the Imperial Navy, for as long as I could remember. We won battles, routed pirates, and delivered precious cargo all under her capable leadership. Yet none of these successful enterprises mattered as I beheld the dread that now contorted the callous beauty of her features.

I had never seen her like this before, and it unnerved me greatly.

Shouts, inhuman shrieks, cries of battle and the the occasional crack of a slung spell were carried towards us over the eerily silent waters. I continued to watch, heart pounding in my chest, as the flashes of light grew closer like a coming storm.

None of us dared to speak. Then, as if expelled from the fog by one of the magical explosions, a being burst forth from the brume. It climbed higher and higher, forcing us to crane our necks. At the apex of its flight it unfurled it's wings and came to an abrupt halt. Golden light issued from it as it hovered there and I felt peace such as I had never known envelope me like a warm blanket. For the first time in my life I was in the presence of what I recognized to be an angel.

Two other forms raced up from the fog after the angel, these with ruddy skin and dark, bat-like wings. They latched on to the golden figure and began dragging it down. I looked on in horror. One of the demons, because that is surely what they were, clambered onto the angels back and bit down into its neck. The other demon clawed ravenously at the angels torso, tearing armor from its body and sinking piercing talons into the flesh beneath.

A third demon rose from the fog as the other two dragged their victim back into it. This one seemed different; more powerful. I prayed that it wouldn't spy our ship in the dark waters but, alas, it spun to face us. The demon let go an ear-splitting screech.

"Men," said Edaline, forcing down the tremor in her voice, "this will be the last time I take up arms with you. It has been a pleasure to serve with such fine seamen."

Her words aroused a plaudit from the deck. The clamor of swords being drawn and crossbows being loaded was momentarily deafening. I drew my own sword and joined in the cries of battle. High above us the first two demons we'd seen had risen to hover alongside the third. They dove, demonstrating speed that could scarcely be believed.

I braced myself. I didn't know much about demons, aside from the stories I was told growing up, but I could already tell that these things were female solely by their lack of apparel. From what I remembered I surmised that these were Qhuezou, diabolic seductresses from the Void. They could take two forms: remarkably attractive human women and the fiends we currently faced.

The she-devils were nearly upon us when a scintillating light had me throwing an arm up over my eyes. I opened them, tears blurring my wounded vision, to see three angelic forms hovering above the Bouyant's bowsprit. The archangel in the center was male, he wore resplendent armor and wielded a sword that looked entirely too large for him—or any man for that matter! The two angels flanking him were females in shimmering golden mail.

The Qhuezou didn't slow their descent in the least. The trio of darkness barreled into the trio of light with an explosive impact. There was little any of us could do as the battle between the quintessential embodiments of good and evil raged on above.

The Qhuezou shrieked and crackling red lightning formed in their palms. The red bolts arced as they sent them hurtling towards the angels, setting the sails alight and all but incinerating the ratlines. One of the female angels caught the brunt of the magical attack. She cried out in a voice that might have been melodious if it wasn't wrought with pain. Her alabaster skin began to blister and pop until she dropped from the sky and was claimed by the gelid waters.

The archangel spun just in time to witness her unfortunate demise. He re-doubled his efforts, fighting with a pitiless savagery I wouldn't have thought a divine being was capable of. One of the Qhuezou fell under his behemoth blade. The other two, seeing their sister fall, targeted him exclusively. He batted one of the she-devils out of the air and brought his sword to bear on the other.

I didn't see what happened next. The Qhuezou he'd knocked from the sky landed on the deck in front of me, but instead of the horror I expected to face I found myself gawking at a stunning and starkly unclad woman with ruby-red hair, violet eyes, and flawless complexion. She stood, nibbled her lower lip enticingly and sauntered towards me.

A slender figure barreled into the woman, sending her and her assailant to the deck and breaking the spell over me. The woman hissed venomously, her teeth elongating into fangs as she began mauling her attacker. The ensuing screams made my skin crawl. I tried to intervene but was thrown back by the demon. I landed hard against the rail. When the she-devil took flight once more I crawled over to the broken and bloodied body of her victim. I was barely able to recognize the mangled face of Edeline Beryl. I knelt by her, gazing over the lacerations adorning her body with growing despair.

"Hines..."

Edeline died in my arms. She had saved my life.

I looked up to see the archangel and the female angel engaged with the leader of the Qhuezou. The she-devil that escaped the deck blindsided the female angel, sinking wickedly sharp claws into the nape of her neck and bringing her down. They struggled for a while but the outcome was clear. The Qhuezou finally delivered a blow that dazed the angel long enough for the demon to impale her of a broken piece of mast.

The archangel faced two now.

The sailors with crossbows began firing at the Qhuezou, the ones that knew about Edeline's death were driven by grief and rage, the others by raw fear. The bolts ripped into the demons. Most of the projectiles went wide but several hit their mark. The lead Qhuezou cackled, mocking our efforts. She was about to send a blast of demonic energy hurtling at the deck when a blinding rift opened in the clouds. Humans and demons alike shielded their eyes. I didn't. It stung at first, but I forced my eyes to stay open.

From the rift of holy light descended a bird that shone with heavenly brilliance. It was large, with a body that seemed to be made of crackling lightning. I knew of this being. This was Illthashore's deity: Avaeos, the Lightning Phoenix.

The remaining Qhuezou screamed as smoke began pouring from their bodies where the light touched —clearly they were unable to abide the deity's presence. They tried to flee but Avaeos loosed a bolt of lightning that reduced them to ash. The Lightning Phoenix didn't pay them a second thought, instead he gestured to the bodies of the fallen angels. On his command they began to float from the dark waters towards the rift. The archangel bowed his head reverently to his lord before charging back to resume battle in the fog.

Avaeos looked at me. *Me.* The only one not dead, unconscious, or hiding their eyes. I was swathed in his light, all my fear and doubt dissolving as if my beloved captain hadn't perished in my arms just moments ago.

I watched as he vanished back into the rift, taking the bodies of his warriors with him. When he was gone, I fell to the deck. My consciousness began to fade and grey spots pervaded my vision.

It was dark and quiet once more. Had what I witnessed really just happened? I glimpsed the butchered form of our former captain and my heart sank. It had indeed been real. My last thoughts before succumbing to the darkness were of angels darting through the sky on silvery wings.

Aethelred

What hadn't fled had died. Animals, mostly livestock, and human caravanners traveling to Sanha lay strewn about him. These poor souls wouldn't have felt much, the Mata'u had risen from the sand with grim intent and siphoned away their lives before most of them realized what was happening. It had probably come from Atset, one of the seven ancient ruins that dotted Udjata. He held its gaze with an equal measure of contempt. There was no reason to fear death, otherwise his end would have already come. No, this creature of nightmares had come to collect him.

"Aethelred," it rasped. Streams of sand continued to sluice off its tattered robes as it spoke. "Kamenwati is disappointed, allowing yourself to be so easily held captive by these humans."

The Mata'u paused to allow its words to sink in. Aethelred watched a scarab crawl out of the creature's mouth, scuttle across its withered gray flesh, and burrow into a hollow eye socket before it continued, "Unfortunately," the dead thing sneered, "our lord prophet still has use of you."

"I allowed myself to be captured," Aethelred countered. "I was being taken to a resistance camp to learn what I might about the movements of the heretics. That is until you ruined all that."

The Mata'u might have smiled, either that or it curled its gaunt lips in anger. Its deathly features made trying to discern many of its facial expressions a useless endeavor.

"It does not matter," said the creature, "you have been summoned back. The day of Apeptsut's resurrection draws nearer."

Aethelred considered his options. He had every intention of returning to the temple with his fellow priests, but not at the discretion of this thing. He held his manacled wrists out before him and, after a pause, the Mata'u reluctantly produced a vial of liquid and tossed it to him. The acid was quick to eat away at the restraints with a caustic hiss. The moment he was free Aethelred strode over to a nearby wagon and sifted through its contents. The staff he was looking for was given to him by the prophet Kamenwati, it allowed him to spew great billowing flames at his enemies. His eyes finally settled on the magnificent black oak staff and, almost reverently, he lifted it from the wagon.

"You're wasting time," the Mata'u said from behind him.

Aethelred spun towards the Mata'u's voice, invoking the fires of the staff as he did. A whirlwind of flames raced towards the creature and engulfed it. There came a shrill, indignant screech from behind the wall of fire.

The Mata'u's eyes flared with anger, "I might have expected this of you! *haty-ek em mi kha!*"

The creature rasped out the words of a spell and vanished. Aethelred recognized the invisibility spell, he was no stranger to this trick. Placing the end of the staff on the ground in front of him, he drew a circle in the sand around himself. A whispered incantation caused the circumference of the circle to erupt in a pillar of fire. Another screech told him that the Mata'u, who no doubt had been closing in for a silent kill, was caught by his circle of protection. Aethelred broke the spell and saw the Mata'u, still invisible but for the flames licking at its robes, thrashing about wildly.

Most undead beings hated fire; it was especially so in Udjata, where the scorching heat desiccated their flesh and made them particularly susceptible to burning magics.

Aethelred knew he had to act fast. Three long strides brought him close enough to deliver a solid whack across the Mata'u's temple, sending it reeling to the ground.

"Traitor!" it hissed.

"I'm no traitor," he replied, "I just don't like being told what to do, especially by the likes of your kind." Aethelred pointed the staff at the now visible creature and once again called forth its fires. Flames poured from the staff and totally enveloped the creature.

Aethelred watched it burn until there was nothing left but crumbling bones.

He glanced around, most of the surrounding wagons and corpses were burning too now. The black smoke would be seen for miles and draw unwanted attention. Aethelred procured a *khopesh* from one of the caravan guards and began his long trek across the desert.

Tsura

There was no mistaking the sound of a Ripper. Its demonic howl resembled that of an infant crying for its mother, but in reality it was a beast created by an ascetic witch in ages past and belonged only in the Void. Since that time Rippers had populated at a tremendous rate and were now used as pets by many sorcerers and necromancers.

To hear the demon's cry in Helsyndel was, to the relief of many, rare. Demons of any kind were not able to reside for long in the mortal plane after being summoned there by magic or dark ritual. The only way a denizen of the Void could remain permanently in Helsyndel was if it passed through the Voidgate or another similar rift between worlds.

Tsurara-onna crouched atop one of the crumbled pillars dotting the area around the Ruins of Shovell, her chiropteran wings furled against the buffeting winds of the blizzard that swept across the plains of Hymult. The sound of an infant wailing reached her ears once more and a smile curled her lips. She saw the long spindly appendages of the Ripper loping towards her even before its full form materialized from the whiteout. Black veins, sprouting from two hollow sockets where its eyes should have been, enveloped the bipedal wolf's entire body. Sinewy muscle rippled beneath its hairless white hide every time its wicked claws sunk into the snow.

Immediately she noted the truncated head held between its jaws. The demon stopped before the pillar she was alighted on and whimpered. Tsura knew by the face of the disembodied head that this man had been an imperial, which without doubt meant that there were more of them in the area. This one the mark of a soldier on his upper left cheekbone.

She hissed through needle-like fangs in anticipation of the coming encounter, "You've done well," she cooed to her pet, knowing that he didn't have long before the magic binding him to Helsyndel ran dry. Already she could see black mist rising from the ground to deprive the demon of his material character.

Tsura turned to the undead men and women fanning out behind the pillar. Most of them had come from imperial camps she'd razed, some from isolated settlements her dead thralls had found in the northern wilds, and others just unlucky enough to have crossed the unholy congregation's path. They stood unmoving but for an errant twitch here and there, their flesh gray and frostbitten from weeks wandering the arctic tundra. Many of the cadavers sported gruesome lesions that barely held back coils of intestine and other visceral matter. One large specimen of a man had had the skin of his torso shorn away to reveal an architecture of broken ribs and frozen muscle tissue.

Voices, muffled by the driving snow, drifted across the tundra towards her. Tsura turned her gaze forward to see dark specks perforate the stark whiteness. They wore heavy fur cloaks over leather armor and each one of them carried either a sword or a spear—save for the crossbowmen. Her keen eyes discerned a platoon of about thirty soldiers emerging from the storm.

Not nearly enough.

The imperials slowed as they neared and dropped into a defensive formation, spearmen in the front, crossbows bringing up the rear, and swordsmen drifting out to the sides to assail their flanks. As they advanced their commander shouted orders that couldn't quite be heard over the din of the wind. It was clear to her though that none of them had yet realized what they marched upon. It *was* possible that her pet hadn't even been seen. All the imperials knew is that something had murdered their comrade, and they were aware of the general direction in which to exact their vengeance.

Tsura stood then, unfurled her wings, and raised her arms high in the air. The imperials who saw her faltered, clearly not expecting a demoness to have risen up before them. With a blood-curdling screech she threw her arms forward. The dead began a slow surge towards the enemy, causing the platoon to grind to a halt as the leading soldiers now saw what they were going up against.

The imperial crossbowmen managed several volleys before the dead fell upon them. Bolts ripped into their risen brethren with little effect, some of the projectiles managed to bury themselves in a corpse's skull, laying it low, but most did nothing to slow the charnel march.

The snowy plain erupted with the cacophony of the living trading blows with the dead. Tsura's army carried weapons brought with them from their previous existence, but there was no real need for them. The dead were just as lethal without iron and steel. Tsura watched in morbid glee as a young warrior was knocked off his feet, four of her minions immediately fell upon him and began raking at his face and any other exposed flesh they could find. The screams of the dying man drew more of the nearby dead, soon his armor had been torn off and ravenous mouths tore at his stomach.

Tsura's eyes turned to another bout not far from the grisly scene. This skirmish, however, seemed to be taking a turn for the worst. Two women, both wielding swords, had their backs to one another and were gradually cutting through her ranks. Already there was an impressive number of bodies accumulating at their feet. Tsura let loose a keening wail and leapt from the pillar, she snapped her wings open and glided down like death from above.

The imperial women noticed too late as she slammed into one of them and bit deeply into her neck. The distraction allowed the dead to quickly gain the upper hand and overtake the other woman still on the ground. Tsura cackled and threw the twitching body, held easily aloft with only one arm, into the nearest throng of corpses.

Every time the demoness saw her corpses being overrun she would interject and change the tide of battle. The imperials couldn't keep up with her and didn't have a leg up against her ability to swoop in, wreak havoc on their forces, and then disappear. All they could do was watch the dead turn their brothers into thralls as Tsura picked off the only warriors amongst them who might have given them a chance. Soon it wasn't so much a battle for the soldiers as a struggle to retreat from their own fallen comrades.

Tsura hovered in the air, looking down on the red snow beneath her and the bodies too mangled to turn. It had almost been too easy to crush this platoon, but she knew full well that her victory here had to be taken with a grain of salt. The Empire was a mighty foe.

"Leave none to return and warn the rest!" the demoness shouted to her army, who eagerly obliged the command.

"Tsura!"

Tsura wrenched herself around to look down at a man that had appeared behind the battle. He wore white robes embroidered with a gray trim, in his right hand he carried a sleek staff and in his left a small book.

"Who are you?" she snarled at the blue-eyed intruder.

"I have not come to fight," he said calmly, "but instead to warn you that your evil taint on this land has not gone unnoticed."

Several of the dead took note of him and began shambling away from the dying imperials.

"The acolytes of Sentus will not stand for your filth pervading here," his tone had grown more serious. "The Abbot challenges you to come for us, he wishes to see the power of a Qhuezou for himself. And if not then we will come for *you*."

Tsura threw her head back in a peal of deranged laughter, "You can't be serious, *old man*."

The monk, or so she assumed as much, shrugged. It was an oddly copacetic gesture for a man nearly surrounded by the living dead. "If you're that confident than I'm sure you will have no trouble killing us all."

Tsura said nothing, convinced that the man was about to be slaughtered by her minions. At the last second though he tore a page from his book and threw it to the howling winds. In an instant he vanished, leaving her to wonder what curious magical properties the book possessed. Tsura bared her fangs in the demonic equivalent of a grin. This was too enticing to pass up, there was no way she could just let such a challenge go unanswered.

With a new imperative she directed her army west towards Sentus, where the Sentus Priory stood at the foothills of the great northern mountain.

The rest of Illthashore could wait a little longer.

Iceclaw Cave

There were some who said that northern Illthashorian winds were the coldest that ever blew —or at least that's what Kaaj had heard, but he would beg to differ!

His robes, wrapped tightly around him, and the heavy cloak he wore atop them seemed scarcely enough to stave off the bitter, biting chill of the blizzard whipping down from the mountains north of Aldrithaw Castle. Whoever it was that claimed the coldest winds belonged to Illthashore had clearly never been to Neverthaw.

Kaaj and his fellow monks had traveled into the north to bring food and supplies to the settlements there, as well as visit a temple built by the grandmasters of old called The Brumal Sanctuary. It was constructed to be a place of pilgrimage for the monks of both Whiteflame and Whitewind Abbey. There they would burn incense and pay homage to Sevastyan Adragain, the founder of the abbeys, and also to Aloysius Silas, Hero of Neverthaw, who had long ago slain the notorious Blackbeast and freed Saint Aleron, a holy figure in Neverthaw, from his icy prison.

The weather had taken a turn for the worse towards the end of their stay at the temple, and now he feared that they would not outrun the sweeping gale. Even now he could barely see his brothers through the heavy flakes falling from the sky.

He increased his pace, trudging through the accumulating snow, legs burning from the exertion and frozen half to death. With each passing minute the storm seemed to worsen exponentially until he could see no more than a few feet ahead—never mind his fellow monks.

Hungry, exhausted, cold, and fretting the worst, it was all he could do to muster the will to press on through the blizzard. The driving wind froze the moisture from his breath onto the scarf he had wrapped around his face, and the exposed skin around his eyes stung as the snow pelted him mercilessly.

It wasn't long until the grim realization that he was no longer following his brothers settled in, and it was with a sinking feeling of dread, perhaps denial too, that he found the strength to pick up his pace. The snow had effectively covered their tracks, however, and it was only a guess as to whether or not he was going the right way.

Eventually, knowing that he was well and truly lost, Kaaj stumbled upon a yawning cave. He stood at its mouth, wondering if it were better to stay outside and freeze to death or be torn apart by whatever might be dwelling within. Inclement weather was only one of the many dangers those who lived on Neverthaw needed to be wary of. Wuhlfs, behrs, yeti, and even werewolves this far north were a looming concern. Any one of those creatures, he knew, would be happy to make a meal of him.

Figuring that he may not feel much if he were to become a yeti's dinner, being so numb already anyway, and wanting nothing more than to be free of the cruel wind, he made his way into the cave.

The relief from the wind was instant, but it was some time later, spent huddled in a corner of the cave, until he was able to feel a vestige of heat returning to his body. Violent shivers wracked his frame at first, but with practiced breathing, curling up into himself, and simple survival tricks he was able to regain some control. When his fingers finally regained some dexterity he procured a torch from the small pack of supplies he carried and lit it by striking some flint off the stone. Fire made the process of warming up much quicker.

When he was ready he decided to delve farther into the cave. During his initial reconnaissance he'd found that there was a tunnel that led deeper underground. Danger lurked everywhere in Neverthaw, but at least it would be warmer farther in and he couldn't stay where he was in case something else decided to wander in, as he had.

With the flaming brand held aloft he steeled his

resolve and began making his way deeper in. The footing in the cave was nothing to be desired, and it was slippery, but he otherwise had little trouble navigating the subterranean passage.

Time lost its meaning, but between the heat of his torch, the exertion, and being out of the storm, he was no longer bitterly cold.

He came upon a few collapsed tunnels. Fortunately, there were alternate passages he could use to avoid the more dangerous areas—or having to go back altogether. He began to wonder if he should just hunker down for the night when he saw a curious feature in the winding tunnel ahead. There was a section of wall that turned inwards at a sharp angle, forming a narrow passage. Kaaj stopped and squinted into the darkness, holding his torch out to the side and behind him so that it did not hinder his vision. From within the passage emanated the lambent glow of torchlight!

Kaaj crept forward, maintaining a cautious awareness of his surroundings. He heard nothing from within the tunnel, but without a doubt he was not alone in this place. The firelight ruled out a wild beast, but bandits or Aldrithic goblins were not out of the question.

By the grace of Saint Aleron, there were neither none of those things in the chamber beyond. The passage was not long and he could see through to a small chamber where a woman, bound in chains affixed to the wall behind her, slumped against her restraints. Two standing braziers burned lazily on either side of her. She appeared to be dead.

Kaaj squeezed through, holding his torch in front of him in case of any surprises. None came. He stood there for a moment on the other side, assessing the unremarkable chamber — other than its occupant — and listening intently.

He could hear breathing, though it was subtle and difficult to pick up over the soft crackle of the fires. It was the woman. She was alive! He hurried over to her, stopping just outside arms reach, and crouched down to better look at her. She wore leather armor beneath a cloak of fur draped across her shoulders and an Imperial sword, still in its scabbard and with the leather strip still clasped over the hilt, hung from her side—had she not tried to fight back against whoever did this to her? Was she ambushed and didn't have the chance to defend herself?

With few clues to answer the questions roiling in his head, Kaaj almost didn't notice her head lift to regard him. When he did lock eyes with her he gave a start and stumbled back, falling onto his rear. She scrutinized him with mesmerizing emerald eyes that bore straight through him. He couldn't seem to tear his gaze away until her eyes softened and he was released from her spell, at which point he felt as if she'd already extraught his deepest thoughts.

"Who are you?" she asked, her silky voice echoing loudly around them.

"My-my name is Kaaj," he stammered, still trying to make sense of the situation.

She said nothing so he continued, "I came into this cave seeking shelter from the storm outside. You are an Imperial?"

The woman nodded, making her charcoal hair shimmer in the warm light. "My patrol and I were tracking a necromancer named Kilaptoewich. We were attacked by goblins riding boars. I was knocked unconscious before I could even draw my blade..." she trailed off, evidently ashamed, "and when I woke I was here. My name is Tourmaline."

"Do you think the necromancer had anything to do with this?" he asked, thinking it strange that goblins would leave her alive and chained up deep in a cave.

It was entirely possible that they'd been instructed to do so, or else Tourmaline wouldn't be alive. Goblins were cruel and malicious creatures. Often, when tribal war parties ambushed travelers or raided caravans, they would kill the men and take the women and any shiny loot back to their lairs. Male goblins were not graced with intelligence, but they understood the value of sparkly things and female captives. Goblin females were less common and generally remained in the lairs, filling the roles of shamans, haruspices, and priestesses.

"No, not likely," she replied. "I think it was rotten luck. Can you help me out of these chains?"

Kaaj nodded and glanced about, considering how he might perform such a task. If he could lift the braziers off their stands he could heat the chain, let it cool, and then strike the hopefully weakened metal. He did just that, careful not to burn himself, and when the chain cooled he used Tourmaline's sword to try and break the links, but to no avail. He heated the chain once more, and once more he swung with all his might. This time the chain did give way. He did the same for her other arm. The sound of metal hitting stone rang uncomfortably in the silence.

When she was free she sat there for a moment, rubbing life back into her limbs. The chains still clinging to her manacled wrists clinked as she moved, but at least she was no longer bound to the cave.

"Thank you," she said when she finally stood.

This woman was young, he realized, in her late twenties he guessed. She stood a head shorter than he did and carried herself with the poise of a warrior who had been trained, and learned discipline, from a young age.

"We should go," he said, "your captors will be back before long."

Kaaj made for the chamber's only exit but realized, as he neared the narrow passage, that the tunnel beyond the chamber did not appear to be as it was when he entered. Instead of bending to the right, as it aught to have, the mouth of the narrow passage hooked left into a larger tunnel that led deeper into the cave.

He glanced back to find Tourmaline coming up behind him. "This place plays tricks on the mind," she explained, seeing his confused expression. "One could wander in these tunnels for days. I was somewhat conscious on the way in and tried to keep track of our path. Alas, the way was too winding and I lost my bearings."

"Even so, I have a good sense of direction," she went on, "I can get us out of here."

Deciding he had no better option at the moment other than to trust her, and believing that she would not lead him astray after he'd saved her, Kaaj relented to letting her take the lead.

They wound through tunnel after tunnel, having to crawl sometimes on their bellies or climb sharply angled sections of stone to higher ledges. Kaaj warmed again as they traversed the subterranean halls, his breathing growing heavy as he expelled large cones of vapor into the cool, stagnant air. Tourmaline, one the other hand, moved with the grace of a cat and appeared not to be bothered by the difficult terrain whatsoever. More than once he found her waiting for him to catch up.

"Are you sure you know where you are going?" he huffed, closing the distance between them as she watched him with a trace of amusement.

"Sure enough," she replied, "do you feel that?"

Kaaj stood there, letting his senses take over. He did indeed feel something—air. A current! The air in this part of the cave was not stagnant! And where there was airflow there was an exit.

Spurred on by the thought of freedom, the pair picked up their pace. Kaaj began to sense a gradual rise in the tunnel's slope and knew that they were ascending from the lower passages. Trekking uphill wore on him even more though, and soon he was making frequent stops to catch his breath while his nimble guide, of course, was nearly out of sight. A while later he managed to catch up to her again and they stood there together, staring at the sunlight glinting through a yawning exit fifty or so paces away.

Tourmaline beamed from ear to ear, "Didn't I tell you I would get us out?"

"That you did," he chuckled, still breathing heavily. "That you did."

He went to place a grateful hand on her shoulder but found only air as his hand fell past where it aught to have rested. Surprised and off-balance, Kaaj retracted his hand and shot a wide-eyed look at the Imperial woman. He could see now in the faint glow of the sun that her form was ever so translucent. Naturally he backed away, but immediately regretted doing so after seeing her hurt expression. She would not harm him, in his heart he knew that.

"Thank you for helping me," she said, "your kindness is a hard thing to come by these days. Had you not at least tried to free me, if you had left me to my fate or sought to take advantage of my condition, you would have wandered these tunnels endlessly. I have seen more lost souls turn a blind eye to my plight than I would have thought possible."

Kaaj said nothing, though he did relax. He hung on her every word, trying to look at her and not through her — assuming the latter to be rude.

"The story I told you was not a lie," she went on, "I was hunting a Necromancer with my fellow soldiers, I was captured by goblins and dragged here, and I was chained up down there to await my doom. But in truth, they did return...and I did die. My fate was unspeakable, and as I lay there in those last awful moments I swore that I would not let anyone else be lost in these wretched depths so long as they were kind of heart, as you were."

Kaaj nodded to her, still in shock. What else could he do? He wanted to go to her and throw his arms around her, tell her everything would be alright; comfort her for as much good as it would do. But no, she was already dead and there was nothing he could do to change that, and so his heart broke as he watched a tear trail down her incorporeal cheek.

"Knowing that there is still good in Helsyndel, even all the way out here in the wilds of Neverthaw, brings me a measure of peace."

"Is there anything I can do for you?" he asked.

Tourmaline shook her head, "Not for me," she replied, "but for yourself. Go, find your way, I cannot leave this place. Not yet. The sun shines and the storm is over. See to it that you get home."

His heart broke again, knowing that to go home would never again be something she would be able to do. She would continue to subsist here, existing yet not real; alone. He stood for a moment longer, grasping for some semblance of reconciliation and searching for words that refused to be found.

Tourmaline smiled, recognizing the turmoil raging within him, and the dam of his thoughts broke. Relief flooded him because he knew then, beyond doubt, that she would be alright. Tourmaline had chosen this existence. She could have gone to the hereafter, but that was not her path. Not yet. This woman would save many more before she found eternal rest, and in knowing that she was at peace.

Kaaj thanked her and set out towards the cave's exit. His fellow monks had likely already made it back to the abbey and sent a search party. They may find him wandering, he thought, but also they might not. No matter, he knew the way.

He breathed deeply, inhaling a lungful of the

sweet mountain air, and walked into the light.

"There are very few who have escaped the inevitable conclusion that we all face at the end of our mortal lives. The fear of death is all too common among every race in Helsyndel, and many cultures share different views of what comes after. But one can never truly die, for their memory will live on and the impacts they made during their lives, however subtle, will have changed the course of fate for others like ripples in a pond. The waters of life are never still. It would be far worse, I think, to have never existed at all, or more terrible yet to have lived a life that will be forgotten. Our actions echo through time long after we are gone, and so we should conduct ourselves accordingly."

- Abbot Jarlan Hyroniemus,

prelate of Whiteflame Abbey

Bone Island

"Why is it called Bone Island?"

The old man, also the boy's grandfather, glanced up from his work on the mangled fishing line and gazed out to the distant silhouette of land on the water. "Many ships have run aground there," he explained, "most pirates, some imperial vessels, and the odd galleon. All aboard perish."

"The shores of the island," he paused then, considering whether his grandson, thirteen years of age, was old enough to hear the rest—he would learn of the island eventually, he decided, "are littered with the skeletal remains of the sailors stranded there. It is said many warriors and heroes have gone to the island to prove their mettle."

He had the boy's rapt attention.

"None have returned," he continued. "As many locations on Helsyndel do, the island has a strange energy about it that allows the dead to walk like the living. Those who sail past under clear skies say they can see skeletal sentinels keeping watch on the bluffs. They are unable to approach, however, because a feeling of dread keeps them at bay."

The boy shivered, his eyes locked on the island, "Then how do they get close enough to run aground in the first place?"

"Storms, fog, poor seamanship. No man or woman in their right minds would go to that place willingly."

"You just said heroes and warriors do."

"Aye, I did. I also never accused them of being in their right mind."

The boy shifted back a little in his cross-legged position atop a large stone.

The old man laughed, "Don't worry yourself, my boy. The undead cannot leave the island, or else the magic that gave them un-life would wear away. What we need to worry about is this fishing line. Here," he tossed a tangled section to his grandson, "unravel that. Don't tell your mother that I tell you such stories. I'd rather swim to the island myself if you ever did!"

That drew a smile from the boy, who had already gone to work on the line.

There had, of course, been a few lucky survivors that had returned from Bone Island, else where would the stories have come from? That though, thought the old man, was a story for another day.

The Realm of Obscurity

Journal Excerpt

The mind is a wicked thing. Order and law are illusions we use to protect ourselves from ourselves, without which the intrinsic frailty of our minds would consume us. There is a tenuous line, like a delicate strand of silk, that separates what we consider sanity from madness. Our servile deference to the powers greater than ourselves is testament to our fears and trepidations. Madness is ever present, lurking in the shadowy corners of our psyche like a shadow out of the corner of one's eye. The only thing containing this madness, in whatever form it may come, are the fantasies we have built around us.

The Realm of Obscurity, written by *The Mage*; Imperial Archives

The Bearer of Darkness

Journal Excerpt

In all of Helsyndel's abundant history, never has there been an event so profound as the appearance of the Deadraisers.

Nobody believed there could exist beings of such nefarious power, and never have I thought a human capable of such wanton cruelty. Not even the priests of Avaeos could rival these dark marauders.

The moment the first Deadraiser set foot in the verdant lands of western Illthashore, the world was plunged into an inexorable twist of fate.

The Deadraisers have had a hand in shaping our history since ancient times, and despite their self-destructive ways, they will continue to influence the machinations of Helsyndel far into the future.

But, as it always has, power begets power, and there will always be stalwart individuals to challenge the darkness.

Eris Draylan - Excerpt from *The World*
Imperial Archives

Babbling Brook

There is an old ghost town to the north called Babbling Brook. The name was given to it because of the pleasantly babbling stream that flows down from the mountains, on whose foothills the village was built. Few venture there now, and the ones who do only do so because they possess a suicidal curiosity — or perhaps they were dared.

Stories are told of a demoniac wind that blows down off the mountains and through the town. Those present during this phenomenon often speak of hearing ephemeral voices borne by the wind as it sweeps past the olden brick chimneys, lichen encrusted gables, and through derelict alleys. They even tell of the horrid shapes of demons that haunt their peripherals, and sinister eyes leering from the shadows cast by neglected masonry and rotting timber — though how embellished those stories are is uncertain.

The most common belief is that angry mountain

spirits murdered the citizens of Babbling Brook. However, in more educated circles, it is said that Firn, Goddess of the North Wind, swept through the town as a deathly gust that stole the life from the unfortunate souls that called that accursed place home. Nobody knows why Firn would do such a terrible thing, but gods are often fickle beings.

Those who believe the latter tale know that it is not angry mountain spirits who occasionally visit the ill-fated village, moaning in the mid-night winds, but the bitter souls of the deceased villagers who still seek justice for the lives that they were so mercilessly robbed of.

There was once a man who even claimed to have seen oil lamps flickering between the trees as he approached the village. He hurried through the surrounding woods, spurred on by a cautious excitement, thinking that there were others there as well. But when he arrived the town was inexplicably dark. Darker even than the gibbous moon above should have allowed. He stood motionless, a gut-wrenching dread rooting him to the spot, as a ghastly breeze wafted through Babbling Brook. With it the wind brought a sepulchral chorus that turned his blood to ice. The man fled then, gibbering later that evening about the waters of the stream turning to blood and wraiths chasing him through the forest.

It would not be for many years until a brave few discovered a cellar beneath one of the oldest houses, and the tunnel therein leading to an unhallowed shrine beneath the village. In this unholy shrine walked the shriveled corpses of all the villagers that once inhabited Babbling Brook. The villagers shambled about the halls of the subterranean shrine, plagued with the insatiable hunger of the undead.

They were put to rest with axe and blade. What those few who ventured into the evil catacombs found afterwards could not be described in any words that could make sense to those who hadn't seen for themselves. Needless to say, they did not emerge from that place with the same vigor and zest for life that they entered with. They carried out the rest of their lives with a mournful disposition that deeply disturbed those around them.

Babbling Brook has remained untouched since that awful night, its existence slowly fading into legend and frightful bedtime stories. The dead are only remembered by those who cannot erase those horrifying tales from memory, and who still hear the gossamer whispers of those freed souls on the wind.

Umeko

"Ocoya? Yes, Ive seen it. Its a beautiful land. Everything inspires a sense of awe and serenity, from the temple cities to the breathtaking countryside."

\- Markus Valens, explorer

Illthashorian northern winds were some of the coldest in Helsyndel—colder even than the glacial winds of Neverthaw, or so it was said. Umeko Kitagawa considered herself resilient to the elements but, as the schooner named Tailwind glided gently across the freezing waters east of Gelid Island, she found herself wrapping her cloak tighter about her.

"How did you come to be in Pinnacle?" asked the captain, who had earlier introduced himself as Salder, his words shattering the tranquil morning silence. "You're from the land far north of here, isn't that right? Ocoya? Forgive me for prying, but I've never exchanged more than a nod with an Ocoyan, and he seemed none to friendly at the time."

Umeko turned from the prow and walked along the deck to take up a new position at the port-side rail, looking out to the sun rising over the distant mountains, "That's right," she said. Her Helsyndilian was by no means good, but she could ask and answer basic questions. She didn't quite know how to explain her circumstances—running from her duties as a woman of the royal family back home in Heodo, bound to marry a man against her will and forced into a sedentary life—but luckily a whale surfaced very near to the boat before she had to, drawing Salder's attention away from the conversation.

The few other crew members milling about began to prepare for port. Umeko could begin to see the northern Helsyndilian coast on the horizon, lit by the sun's golden rays. Along the coast rose the spires of Helsydel's north-most city: Asperia. It was here that Salder would drop his Ocoyan cargo, loaded back in Pinnacle where Umeko had bartered passage on the Tailwind, and pick up goods to head north again the next day.

Foreigners were still not allowed in Ocoya, but the Ocoyan noble families had nonetheless, though not without much deliberation, sought to establish trade with Helsyndel. It wasn't long afterwards that a handful of Umeko's people had ventured into Helsyndel themselves, despite the continued occlusion of all others from their own continent—save for one man, an explorer named Marcus Valens. This was regarded with some suspicion by the Imperial Army of Helsyndel, but the exotic wares offered by the Ocoyan's had thus far repressed any real cynicism.

Umeko knew her people meant no harm, they were merely set in their cloistered ways. Emperor Nakayama Meiji, sovereign of Ocoya, was nothing if not a man of honor.

The whale followed the boat for a while longer before suddenly making itself scarce. Umeko went from rail to rail searching for him—or her—but to avail. Disappointed, she made her way down to the cargo hold, where her lodgings consisted of a small cot and her personal effects, to find some warmth for the final stretch of their journey.

She had barely made it a handful of steps into the hold when the schooner bucked fiercely, throwing her to the floor with a few barrels and crates. Had the whale bumped into them by mistake? Umeko scarcely gained her footing when she was pitched sidelong into a stack of crates as the ship heaved again. Frantic cries could be heard from above once her ears stopped ringing. Umeko made for the stairs to see what was going on when a guttural roar set her back on her heels. The cries of the men abated for several heartbeats; ice gripped her heart.

Instinct told her to dive towards the prow of the schooner seconds before a massive octopean tentacle crashed through the deck and into the cargo hold, not quite bisecting the boat but certainly sealing her fate. The tentacle retracted, dragging with it screaming crew members and making way for a rush of icy seawater. Umeko was only afforded a brief glimpse of the monstrous octopoid before the boat rocked so violently she was thrown out of the gaping hole in the hull and into the Iceing Sea. Umeko gasped as the sea wrapped its bitterly cold fingers around her. She knew she had very little time before disorientation and unconsciousness set in, assuming the boat-destroying creature didn't kill her first.

The monster was gargantuan, its hide was rubbery like a squid and from its torso, which currently rose above the water, sprouted four two-taloned arms. Its head was nothing more than a bulbous lump on its body with a jagged row of razor-sharp teeth above which rested four gelatinous black eyes.

Umeko watched in horror as several tentacles rose from the water like serpents, wrapping around the schooner and reducing it to mangled timber. The sailors who weren't crushed between the planks of the boat dove into the sea where they were dragged under by smaller tentacles to drown.

The creature, apparently satisfied with its work, waited a moment before sinking back into the depths it called home. Umeko floated as still as she could manage with violent shivers wracking her body. Salder's corpse bobbed nearby. Umeko tried to focus on the floating cadaver of the captain but her vision was beginning to blur. Everything seemed to be moving in slow motion and her limbs struggled to obey her commands, already she had lost most of the feeling in her extremities.

It was hard to tell how long she had drifted before she felt metal hooks slide under each arm and lift her as gently as possible from the water. She heard voices but they seemed so far away, somebody undressed her—purely out of necessity—and wrapped her in several wool blankets while an attempt was made to rub life back into her limbs. Umeko was able to pick up bits of conversation as her consciousness teetered on the brink, things such as: "Lord Volvoski will want to know", "must be seen by a healer", and "child of Cyrqyx, here?".

Finally, after what seemed like an eternity, Umeko felt the spark of life return to her and knew that she could let darkness wash over her without fear of never waking up. The last thing she heard before slumping into oblivion was a man shouting: "make for Asperia!"

Crooks Hollow

There is a place in the woods north-east of Greyelo that is only spoken of in hushed tones, and only behind closed doors or discreetly over the rims of pints in noisy taverns. It is a place of malignant evil and frighteningly unnatural occurrences. What was once a thriving farmstead called Crooks Hollow had, over several generations, become a cursed plot of land that few dared to tread upon. The home on the property, which once stood proud atop a nearby hill, had long since toppled under the weight of its own rotting timber. Nobody knows the true nature of the plight that befell Crooks Hollow, and the topic is never broached in open discussion, but it is suspected that the family fell grievously ill or went mad.

Or both.

Those who do venture past on the road, purely out of necessity, speak of horribly disfigured scarecrows in the cornfield that seem to watch them from the weathered poles on which they dangle, their tattered grins betraying a malevolent sentience that chill those passing by to the bone. Leering barbed devils are seen too, on occasion, peering over the shoulders of the scarecrows they possess. The ruddy fiends, whose eyes are lit from within by an eerie glow, will even stand along the edge of the field at night as if daring onlookers to come close — as they do not seem to be able to leave the property themselves.

Nobody knows where exactly these devils came from. Perhaps from some unknown plane of existence whose planar stratum infringed upon the physical plane, creating an ethereal bridge and linking the two worlds to some degree. Such occurrences have been documented before, places like The Boneyard, the Voidgate, the Veiled Summit in Neverthaw, and the four elemental shrines are such locations.

Foolish youths have dared each other to approach the accursed cornfield; they quickly discovered the idiocy of their games. Luckily, only a few have gone missing, but this is of no consolation to the families of those lost to that evil place.

A little girl once wandered into the cornfield with her favorite doll, her most cherished possession. She was, fortunately, not one of the children who was taken by the devils within, but her doll slipped from her grasp as she ran crying from the Stygian maze. The girl later lamented the loss of her toy, though there are those who claimed to have seen the scraggly figure of a child's doll clambering up to perch upon the shoulders of the scarecrows, wherefrom it surveyed the field with malicious intent.

Perhaps the most awful manifestation of the crop are its phantasmal keepers. On evenings when the moon is full they can be seen tending to the farmstead. At first glance they appear as normal as you or I, but their faces are a sickening mockery of human likeness. Many flee upon witnessing the horror of their countenance, for their eyes have been plucked out by the barbed devils and their mouths haphazardly sewn shut. The keepers of the crop don't themselves seem evil, their tortured expressions plead for a release from their torment, but their ghastly features turn away all who might have offered aid.

Crooks Hollow has become a place of the damned. Never again will it bear the wild flowers that blanketed the farm in spring or hear the songs of the birds that once called the barn's rafters home. Nothing grows there now. No wildlife nests in the gnarled, cankerous trees or burrows in the noxious soil.

Only darkness reigns in Crooks Hollow, where the scarecrows grin and the devils leer.

Always watching.

The Banneret Vanguard

The first time I witnessed the Banneret Vanguard in action was at sea. Our vessel, the HMIS Reliance, captained by the renowned Bryce Martin, had been tasked by Emperor Herman Troil alongside the HMIS Adept to defend an Ocoyan galleon north of Asperia and west of Pinnacle.

One of my crew-mates shook my shoulder and pointed to the skies, where puffy white clouds blanketed the heavens. At first I didn't see anything, but then a bird flitted between the clouds. Then another. I narrowed my gaze and realized they were not birds, but gryphons. Their silent majesty gave testament to the incredible power of the creatures. I squinted harder and saw armored shapes atop the gryphons, glinting in the rays of sunlight, as they banked to and fro.

Eventually, as we suspected it would be, a pirate

flag was spotted on the horizon. Bryce immediately raised the alarm, having the archers stand at the ready and the crewmen prepare for boarding.

We needn't have bothered.

The pirate vessel was able to approach close enough so that we could see the rapscallions jeering at us from deck—but that was as far as they got. Like a rain of death from above, the winged warriors descended on the ship in a pernicious gale.

The pirates were as surprised as we were. The Banneret Vanguard fell upon them in a rush of feathers, talons, and steel. They were ill prepared for the assault and soon a crimson layer of blood covered the wooden planks of their ship. In a matter of minutes it was over; only one gryphon floated in the waters beneath the ship.

The Reliance was not needed, it seemed, and even Bryce, who stood at the bowsprit, wore an expression of bewilderment as the slaughter unfolded across the surf. I saw the Adept sailing alongside the Ocoyan galleon not far off, ushering them past the battle and into safer waters.

From the clouds, very suddenly and startling many of the men, descended a large gryphon and its rider, who wore a full suit of gleaming armor. "Who is Captain Bryce?" the sky-knight asked by way of greeting, speaking in an authoritative baritone.

Bryce strode towards the rider, showing no fear in the face of the great creature on his ship. The gryphon's talons dug small furrows into the planks, forever a reminder of its presence on the Reliance. "I am," he declared.

"It's an honor, Captain," said the rider. "I would ask that you go to the pirate vessel and peruse it for anything useful to the empire. Our riders will continue scouting the horizon for any more of them." He watched the distant HMIS Adept and the Ocoyan ship for a few heartbeats. "Our guests seem to be in good hands."

Bryce nodded, "Of course, without delay. Anything of interest to the empire will be brought to Skell when next we make port."

"Good," the gryphons straightened up and spread its wings, which easily spanned the deck from port to starboard. "For justice!"

With that, gryphon and sky-knight took to the air with a powerful gust and a mighty screech that would have struck fear into the most nefarious of pirates captains. I would later learn that his parting words was the customary mantra of the Banneret Vanguard.

Bryce began giving commands after the wind died down. We all hustled to carry out his orders, but I couldn't shake the images of the gryphons from my mind.

I was astounded.

The empire was truly a formidable force.

The Siren

Sweeping sheets of rain cascaded from the night sky.

The colossal cavern yawned before him, daring those foolish enough to believe themselves brave to delve into its cyclopean depths. He was no longer able to hear the waves breaking on the shoreline rocks behind him or smell the briny scent of the sea on the air. Instead, he heard…a voice. It called to him from the darkness ahead, but it was distorted, as if he were holding a seashell to his ear. It was contorted; distant; droning.

It sang to him.

He took a step forward, then another.

The soles of his bare feet met the cold, slimy rock of the cave with wet padding sounds and his breath came shallow.

He was drenched, shivering, hungry, exhausted, and lost, but none of that seemed to matter at that moment. Only the voice mattered. That exquisite, mesmeric melody drifting to him from the primordial deep. He could scarcely remember how he ended up here, only that it had something to do with the storm raging outside.

Lightning arced across the sky behind him, casting harsh light into the cave and illuminating pools of water scattered among the stalagmites. Things moved in the pools, disturbed by the intense flashes from outside their murky home. They possessed bodies akin to tadpoles, but their arms, torsos and ichthyic heads appeared unnervingly human. Some broke the surface of their shadowy pools to regard him with pallid, unblinking eyes before sinking back beneath the surface.

He trod on, towards the voice.

The piscine things watched him as he passed but showed no aggression towards the strange biped creature intruding on their home. Some chose not to regard him at all and sunk deeper beneath the water in an attempt to hide from the garishly bright lightning.

Thunder echoed loudly off the cavern walls, but he paid it no mind.

He only had ears for that beautiful serenade, sung just for him.

Soon the cavern floor rose up, leaving the pools behind. It was hard to see now through the darkness, at least with his inadequate human eyes, but that was not a concern to him. He didn't need them anymore. His ears knew the way.

The storm seemed a faraway thing now. The voice had become clearer, richer, more beautiful. It was the voice of a woman. She called to him, beckoning him from his misfortune, promising only warmth and ecstasy so long as he succumbed to her call.

He found her sitting on a dais in the middle of a stone chamber vaster even than the cave's entrance. A bizarre bioluminescence from the stalactites above offered enough light for him to see her well enough, and land sakes alive was she a sight to see!

The woman's long, wavy hair, the color of ale,

cascaded down her unclothed, sylphlike form and framed a face hewn from the heavens. She smiled at him and suddenly his legs were no longer his to command. He lost himself in her inky eyes, enraptured by the salacious intensity of her gaze.

So driven by his desire was he that he failed to notice that the lower half of her body was that of a long, streamlined tail with lucent lateral fins.

He dropped to his hand and knees as he neared her and crawled the rest of the way to where she sat. With palsied hands he reached up and took hold of her slender waist, slowly wrapping his arms around her. The woman, still singing in that lovely voice, lay his head down in her lap.

From behind him rose the spear-like tip of her tail, angled down towards him with malicious intent. The woman smiled again, this time revealing a multitude of long, pointed fangs.

She ceased her song.

He took in a sharp breath, waking with a start from the trance she had placed upon him.

Confused, he lifted his head from the mucousy skin of her lower half and cast about the chamber. Finally, his eyes turned upwards to gaze into her sable orbs. His face drained of color at the sight of what she had become. No longer was she the breathtaking vixen that had lured him to this primeval grotto. Now, he saw only death.

The beings in the pools barely stirred as his agonized screams reverberated off the ancient walls of the cavern. They were far more concerned by the nearly constant flashes of light interrupting their slumber.

A clap of thunder split the skies, drowning out the man's final pleading cries.

Aliyah

"Do you suppose the greater mistake was summoning the demon, or expecting it to be grateful?"

Edgard Marsh glanced over the hamlet from the crest of a nearby hill. From their vantage point they were afforded an excellent view of the smoking crucks and thatch-covered bodies—some well beyond recognition—strewn about the area. It hadn't been long since the carnage took place, the lightly falling snow had not yet left a dusting on the things that weren't burning.

He and a younger disciple of the Sentus Priory had been sent by Prior Ulfr Bardawulf to investigate a surge of demonic energy at the foothills of the mountain range to the north. Whatever caused this destruction, however, was gone. As was whoever had summoned the demon. Prohibited magical practices were becoming too commonplace in Illthashore. Likely this was nothing more than a foolish young magician experimenting with dark magic that he—or she—had no business dabbling in. Thankfully, the demon's presence, without practiced hands holding the reigns, would quickly diminish.

But the damage had been done.

"There is nothing we can do here," he said, turning away from the grisly scene.

"Brother Edgard, look!"

He spun back to see the disciple pointing to one of the more in-tact crucks. Something was moving inside.

"Follow me," he instructed, "and keep close."

The white-robed pair trudged cautiously into the devastated hamlet, wary of surprises that may leap from the flames. Nothing accosted them though, and soon they stood at the crumbling entryway of the house. Edgard produced a small book from his robes, just in case.

To his surprise, and surely to the disbelief of the younger monk, a girl no older than ten or eleven winters stepped from the rubble. She was in obvious shock and whatever she had been wearing was little more than rags, offering less than adequate protection from the cold. Edgard saw something in her hazel eyes that he had not seen in a long time: true horror.

"Oh child!" The disciple exclaimed, rushing to wrap his robe around her.

"Wait!" Edgar barked. He stared into the eyes of the child, making certain that this was indeed *just* a young girl and not a demon trying to deceive them. Finally, with confidence, he nodded to the disciple. The young monk draped his robe around her and let the girl climb up onto his back so that he could carry her.

"Ready?" he asked when she was comfortable. The girl nodded, her face half buried in his shoulder.

"What is your name?"

"Aliyah," she said.

Edgard cast about, suddenly on edge being so out in the open and exposed. "Take the girl back to the hill. Do it *now*."

They were not alone.

The disciple didn't hesitate. He recognized the urgency of the tone and knew to do as he was told. His timeliness served him well, for had he lingered a moment longer he would surely have been impaled by any of the eight legs that burst from the flames of a neighbouring home. Edgard had to throw himself to the ground in an evasive roll just to avoid the chitinous appendages. What emerged from the burning timber was something he hoped he would never see again after this day. The arachnid stood at least twenty feet high with legs nearly twice that length and a bulbous purple body patterned with yellow streaks. Edgard stared into its many eyes, fighting back the influence of fear the demon innately projected and preparing himself for battle.

The attack came, but not in the manner he was expecting. What came first was a name that cut through his thoughts like a hot knife, perhaps telepathically conveyed by the demon.

Zhisath, the Shrieker.

Then, he found out why she was called "the Shrieker". Zhisath darted towards the fleeing disciple, using superb tactile sensation to pick up their movement in the accumulating snow. The motion kicked up a flurry that blinded the older monk and overwhelmed his senses with a chilling, scuttling screeching that could only be coming from the monstrous spider.

"Zhisath!"

The demon stopped and spun towards Edgard.

The hairs on his arms and neck stood on end. A novice may not have known what was about to happen, but he did. He tore a page out of the book and held it up before him just as a bolt of lightning shot from the demon's carapace and crackled into the barrier Edgard had raised to protect himself. Two more successive bursts followed the first, preceding the arachnid's furious charge. Edgard used the magical properties of the book to erect a wall of ice between himself and the demon. It didn't hold her back for long, but it was long enough for him to ready his next spell. He was casting before the demon even broke through the wall. A radiant beam of light raced towards the arachnid and enveloped her before fading away to nothing. Zhisath, albeit dazed, looked unharmed. The spell, however, was a success. Dark mist began rising from the ground to claim the demon. Zhisath lunged for Edgard in one final attempt to tear the monk to pieces, but by the time the demon reached him she was no longer a corporeal thing. Edgard watched her collapse to the ground, becoming no more than ash marring the newly fallen snow.

Edgard looked to the hill, where the disciple and the girl stood watching.

There were many tomes at the priory annotating the demons found within the Void, where this arachnid had been summoned from. If he remembered correctly, Zhisath was one of the Zaviwrath. Prior Ulfr would have to be informed of this. In the demonic hierarchy, a Zaviwrath was no lesser demon. It would have taken a compelling summoning ritual to bring something that powerful into Helsyndel. Perhaps the summoner was no novice after all.

Edgard began trekking back towards the pair waiting on the hill, his thoughts roiling.

The world had just become a far more dangerous place.

The Reaper

It was a perfect night for killing.

The only sound in the cold, dark woods was the rustling of leaves in the breeze, but that was more than the three assassins needed to cover their movements as they stalked like black-clad phantoms between the trees, occasionally conveying hand signals to one another. Ahead of them, forty or so paces from the treeline, was the cottage of an Illthashorian politician named Wiscar Brice.

To say that Wiscar was corrupt was an understatement. He had been funneling money into his own coffers meant for communities stricken by food shortages—a crisis that he himself caused so that he could launder the support funds from the empire. When confronted he had, of course, denied the accusations, somehow skirting legal precedents, and run to his cottage just west of Greyelo on the coast.

Caspar Nyx held up a hand to stop the others. The other two assassins, Yadira Raine and a man who refused to go by anything but "Reaper", came to a halt, becoming indistinguishable from the moonlit shadows. They were Shadow Seekers, the emperor's deadliest force. The fact that they were even here, contracted to kill one of Illthashore's own high-profile figures, was a testament to the severity of the situation.

There were always three sent to carry out a contract, no matter how insignificant the target. Wiscar, however, was by no means insignificant. His death would be noticed. Fortunately, there would only ever be speculation as to his demise. When the empire needed someone to disappear, silently and without repercussions, they sent Shadow Seekers.

Caspar signaled to Reaper to begin closing the distance to the cottage. Reaper would be the one to carry out the assassination while Caspar waited close by to offer support, if needed. If Reaper missed his shot, Caspar would not. Not that it would be necessary, he had utmost confidence that Reaper would carry out his mission without fault. Yadira would stay back and observe, as she was the newest of the trio, ready to assail their enemies from afar should the need arise.

Reaper favored the crossbow, which he brandished now with grim intent. He was one of the most lethal men Caspar knew. They'd trained for years together to become Shadow Seekers and ran enough missions to damn near know what the other was thinking.

The briny scent of the sea hit them as they crept closer to the cottage, using boulders and scrub as cover. There was a lantern lit on a desk inside, visible through a window, at which a lone figure sat scribbling on some papers. Caspar, from his angle, couldn't confirm that it was Wiscar, but Reaper, who was much closer, affirmed his suspicions that it was indeed the politician.

It was strange, either he wasn't worried about

reprisal for his crimes, he was too stupid to have hired a security detail, or he *did* have security in place and was arrogantly confident that he was safe. Still, security or not, Reaper's crossbow bolt would shatter the window and bring Wiscar down long before he could be saved.

Unless Wiscar's protection was magical in nature.

Caspar produced a small vial of blue liquid from the folds of his jerkin and tossed it back, swallowing the bitter brew with a grimace. For the next few minutes any magical properties of anything he saw stood out to him like a beacon in the dark. He was able to see an aura back along the treeline around the blade strapped to Yadira's back, and also from a ring that Reaper wore. The ring, he knew, allowed Reaper to see through heavy fogs and other natural obscurities to a degree others could not.

No auras sprung from Wiscar's cottage.

Something wasn't right here.

The auras faded and Caspar saw Reaper looking back at him from the decaying wooden fence encompassing the cottage. His crossbow was loaded and primed to execute the killing shot. Caspar signaled to him to hold. He didn't often ignore his instincts, and right now they were telling him that they'd overlooked something.

Caspar sucked in a breath as a knife was pressed into his side.

"Do not move," came the silky voice of a woman, her words were whispered into his ear like drops of poison. Caspar couldn't believe that she'd been able to sneak up on him!

"Wiscar *will* die," said the woman behind him, "but not until you've heard what I have to say. Oh, and don't speak, Reaper will hear you. Just listen."

Caspar nodded once, careful not to make the movement too sudden. Reaper, he noted, appeared not to have become aware of the exchange. He was preoccupied watching their target. Caspar doubted he could hear the woman anyway. Her gossamer whispers were carried away by the breeze, becoming nothing more than forgotten breaths on the late autumn air.

"Wiscar hired me to protect him," she continued. "He paid more money than most could make in several lifetimes. Unfortunately for him, I don't disagree that he needs to be put to rest. My reason for accepting his contract is to tell you that we've had our eyes on you for quite some time, and to ensure that your mission is a success. Your skill, and Reapers, is wasted working for the empire."

Reaper looked his way again and Caspar felt the knife dig into his side. Once again he motioned for his fellow Shadow Seeker to hold his position.

"Come to Kaleia. Go to The Miner's Pick tavern and ask for the latest rumors. We will find you."

Caspar stole a glance at the treeline, trying to locate Yadira.

"Yadira is fine," said the woman. "She can no more see me than Reaper can."

Caspar slowly held his hand out low to his side and, making sure Reaper was still not watching, communicated a question to the woman in a universal sign language used by professionals of their ilk.

He could *feel* her lips curl into a smile; it sent a shiver up his spine, "We do not have a name. We are the wisps of spider-silk you see on the path ahead. Ghosts that plague the darkest nights, lurking just beyond your perception."

He felt the pressure of the knife ebb away.

Caspar turned quick enough to draw Reaper's attention. The woman was gone, fading into the night as surely as if she'd been dispersed on the wind. He turned back to the cottage to find Reaper regarding him with concern and signaling to make sure everything was alright. Caspar nodded to him and gestured for him to proceed.

Reaper stood with cold determination, leveled his weapon at the window, took aim, and squeezed the trigger. The shatter of a windowpane and the thud of a body hitting the floor immediately followed. He and Caspar returned to the treeline after Reaper made sure the job was done.

Caspar was never in doubt of the outcome of their mission, but the unforeseen meeting, which he would later divulge to Reaper, had unnerved him — not an easy feat. He did, however, intend to find this surreptitious organization.

The woman had presented an interesting prospect.

Not long after they'd gone, the flame of a lantern flickered and died in the breeze let in by a broken window.

Balmelech

Tsurara-onna was not bothered by the cold. It wasn't a magical resistance, as most human adventurers acquired for travel in the frigid north, it was simply that she was not of the mortal plane. She felt it, to be sure, but was not physically hindered by it. She chalked up the innate resistance to her demonic blood as she soared through the blizzard, high above her macabre army. The undead legion was equally unaffected by the bitter winds.

The skies ahead were bleak, but she knew the way. Not by sight, however, not even the eyes of a Qhuezou could peer through this storm. The sense of devoutly religious purity that radiated from the priory was like a beacon in the dark. It sickened her.

So focused was her hatred that she failed to notice the skies beginning to take on an unearthly purple hue, or the pelting snow slowly lifting until only lazy flakes drifted down to alight on her flaxen hair.

Tsura stopped, hovering high above the ground.

Her surroundings looked reminiscent of the Void, but the same mountains still scraped the sky around her—and it didn't snow in the Void.

"Tsurara-onna."

The voice, a deep and grating baritone, came from all around her, as if reverberating off the mountains themselves. She glanced down to where her army should have been; they weren't there. It seemed she had flown into some warped amalgamation of the Void and the mortal plane.

"Tsura," the voice said again, growing in intensity.

Tsura spun in the air and glowered as she came face to face—literally—with a colossus of a demon. The monstrosity's face was that of a bat, but with yellow eyes far more intelligent than those of a flying rodent. Tattered wings that blotted out the skies sprouted from equally massive shoulders, below which six long tentacles draped down its back like a writhing cloak. The demon's arms were corded with bulging muscle and ended in wickedly serrated claws. Tsura noted, too, the demon's lower half, which was that of a human male — or that of a giant one anyway, a fact of which she was unfortunately *very* aware of. The fiend, from the points of his wicked horns, easily contested the nearby mountains in height.

"Balmelech," she hissed.

Balmelech was one of the four supreme demon's whose dominions encompassed all the territories of the Void. They were known also as the chosen of Madreas. This one Tsura least enjoyed the company of. At least his physical form was not truly with her, although this projected phantasm and her altered surroundings were nothing if not attestations to his incredible power.

"Yes," Balmelech replied. "So, the rumors are true. You are here on the mortal plane. How did you manage that?"

"Not your concern," she spat, not taking her eyes off the great demon. If he could warp her reality all the way from the Void, that meant he could hurt her too. "What do you want, Balmelech?"

Balmelech grinned — or at least his approximation of it, "I wish to join your…conquest."

Tsura might have laughed, but she bit her tongue. She hated Balmelech, as all Qhuezou did. Even so, she knew better than to anger him. "I think not," she said instead.

"Oh, come now," he grinned wickedly, making a point to flex his enormous shoulders and stretch out his wings to their full span. "We could have so much fun together," he said as his gaze dropped from her face.

Tsura irately crossed her arms over her bare chest. Qhuezou, much of the time, appeared as strikingly beautiful human females. Their true banshee-like appearance, a form often taken in battle, was truly horrifying, but most Qhuezou could remain in their human forms while aloft, electing to revert only enough to allow a few of their demonic traits to show — such as their atramentous wings and taloned nails. One aspect of themselves they could not hide, however, no matter which form they took, were their violet irises. This identified them as demons in human civilizations, but it was nothing a simple cantrip couldn't hide for a short time.

"I would never release you."

Balmelech stared at her, as if considering whether or not to swat her from the air.

"I will grant you power unlike you've ever seen under the yoke of Lyvithia," he rumbled, speaking of another of Madreas' chosen, the demoness all Qhuezou paid homage to.

"Leave," she gritted. "I will not open the way for you."

Balmelech chuckled again, an infuriating sound. "I will find a way to the mortal plane, Tsura. And if you do not open the Voidgate for me, when I find another way, I will come for you first."

Tsura was about to offer a retort, but the wind had begun battering her once again.

Balmelech was gone.

It was an interesting turn of events, one that she would have to handle cautiously.

With the encounter at the forefront of her thoughts, she continued north.

Kraken Moon

"Not many in Helsyndel know the tale of Scyshyg the Lunar Serpent and the Mystics, trained in the old forgotten magics, that hold him at bay when the moon is full. As well they shouldn't, for Scyshyg is one of the few remaining Elder Beasts whose power rivals that of even the gods. If his existence ever became known, and it was discovered that he would terrorize the Iceing Sea unrivaled if the Mystics ever failed in their duty, hysteria would ensue."

Artizar Sotil, Mystic of the Lunar Monastery

- addressing Lunar Initiates

The nondescript wharf was unlike anything Dederic Graves expected as he and a senior Mystic named Gisela walked towards the tranquil, moonlit expanse of open sea stretching out from the shore. Gisela, he noted, had chosen to wear her hair loose for the excursion. It spilled down her back in silvery waves, almost appearing to become one with the equally luminous runic illustrations on the deep blue robes they wore. She was rather attractive for her age, which he knew to be about twice his own age of twenty-seven winters.

Gisela had warned him not to speak during what the Lunar Monastery headmasters called the Moonrite, but instead to only observe — as one day it would be he standing alone on the wharf with a Lunar Initiate watching him perform the Moonrite.

She held up a hand to signal that he should stay where he was and continued on to stand at the edge of the weathered, crumbling masonry of the derelict wharf. For nearly a full candle-mark they stood waiting and listening to the silently lapping waves of the gelid waters. Then, with terrifying silence, a massive scaled hide slowly breached the water and rose to loom over the lone Mystic. Scyshyg's menacing gaze bore into her as eight horrid tentacle-like appendages snaked past rows of razor teeth to snatch her up and drag her into its maw.

Two rows of scales on either side of its finned

spine began to glow in the light of the moon, and as they did the runic illustrations adorning Gisela's robe also began issuing an eerie blue light. The Elder Beast stopped, seeing the aura enveloping the Mystic, and withdrew the appendages. Gisela spoke to the serpent in an antediluvian language known only to the Lunar Mystics, still relevant solely for the Moonrite, in a voice that was soothing yet carried with it absolute authority. Scyshyg reared back to his full height, illuminated from behind by a moon that suddenly seemed twice its normal size, and rumbled an indecipherable response to Gisela's ancient tongue.

For a moment the Mystics could not move, it was as if their muscles simply wouldn't obey in the presence of this age-old being. In the wake of Scyshyg's primeval power they could not even bring themselves to blink.

Then, it was gone.

It was several long moments after the serpent's descent back into the sea that Dederic finally registered Gisela's hand on his shoulder. She seemed not to have been as affected as he was by the overwhelming presence of Scyshyg.

"It will get easier," she said, the runes on her robes still pulsed with eldritch energy. "The serpent understands the Edocean language, he respects those who can still speak it. These runes counter the dangerous aggression that boils up within him during the full moon."

Dederic nodded, not yet able to find words to respond.

"Come," she tilted her head inland, making her hair shimmer radiantly, "let's return to the monastery. You need to eat something."

Dumbfounded by the awesome experience, he fell into step behind her.

Behind them the ripples from the serpent's parting finally subsided.

Illusions of Gold

"What good is all the riches in Helsyndel if it is not used to see the world?"

        - Accalon Tenabrus, wealthy patrician

Flames crackled and spit, sending sparks high into the crisp night air of summer. Bheren Magnus sat alone on a fallen log, staring into the blaze and listening to the flow of the river on whose bank he had made camp.

He'd left Lersal the day before yesterday, bound for a nameless crypt bordering the region around the volcanic mountain called Harratus. In this sepulcher there was rumored to be treasure beyond imagining, and there were none yet who had been able to claim it. Many fortune seekers had made this same journey as he, never to be seen or heard from again. There was heresay that the crypt was the resting place of one of the forefathers of the enigmatic Helsyn family.

The stretch of a bowstring drew his attention.

"I don't suppose you're going to the same place I am?" he heard a voice from behind him. It was the voice of a woman.

Bheren poked at the fire and cautioned, "I would advise against that."

"Against what?" the woman asked. "Going to the same place as you or having an arrow pointed at the back of your skull?"

He stood slowly, rising to a height that towered over most men, and turned towards the voice. The woman hid in the darkness of the trees, where he could only vaguely see her. "Take your pick. There are many travelers on this road, what makes you assume our destination is the same?" he rumbled.

"I've been trailing you for the past day." There was a distinct pause where he could feel her studying him, "Are you the one they call *Bloodfire*?"

Bheren spread his arms, "Tis I." Perhaps it was his long, thin black beard that she recognized. Or maybe the dark hair that fell past his shoulders. He was one of those people that everyone seemed to remember, and unfortunately the moniker *Bloodfire* was not as inconspicuous as he would like it to be.

The woman stepped out of the shadows. It was a nervy move to reveal herself, but her poise suggested a cocksure attitude. She was no more than thirty winters, about twenty younger than himself. "Keep your arms out, *do not* make any sudden moves."

Her accent sounded Norndish, but her facial features — slim nose, full lips, high cheekbones, and fair complexion — marked her as a woman of the Gelid Isle. Either way, her origins pointed north. She wore her dark auburn hair pinned back in a tousled mess. It was a spitting image of organized chaos.

"Where are you headed to?" Bheren asked her, already suspecting he knew the answer.

Keeping her shot trained between his eyes, she took another slow step toward him, "I seek treasure. And you?"

"It would seem we have similar goals in mind."

She drew back further on the bowstring, her arrow set to fly, "That, my friend, is truly unfortunate — for you. I'm not keen on sharing."

"Before you shoot me," he said, knowing that if he wasn't quick her arrow could easily kill him, "can I ask you a couple questions?"

"If you must," she scoffed — there was that arrogance again.

"What's your name?"

"It doesn't matter."

"Please," he said, turning his palms out in a helpless gesture, "seems like I'm a dead man anyway. At least show me the respect of telling me who is sending me to my grave.""

The woman sighed reluctantly, "Eviri."

"Eviri," he repeated, "thank you."

"Ask your second question," she huffed.

"Of course. Do you want to see why they call me Bloodfire?"

Eviri, eyes going wide, responded by releasing the

arrow, which sailed straight and true through the space between them — too late. The veins along Bheren's body erupted with an inner fire that blinded Eviri and sent her stumbling backwards in a hasty retreat. The projectile burnt up before reaching its target and anything around Bheren was badly singed by the flashfire. It was over as quickly as it began, except for the molten rivers of blood that criss-crossed Bheren's entire body. His tunic and trousers, however, were thankfully intact. For whatever reason, the fire never seemed to affect anything touching his person.

"They call me Bloodfire," he began, weakened from the outburst and panting, "because long ago a demon cursed me with blood that constantly burns within me. It does have its uses though. I suppose the constant pain is a small price to pay."

Eviri coughed and sat upright, blinking repeatedly to clear her vision. "I should have just shot you from the trees," she spat angrily.

He shrugged, reaching a hand down to help her

up, "Is there a reason you didn't?"

Eviri slapped his hand away. Now that she didn't have an arrow knocked in his direction he was better able to take stock of her: she wore a leather corselet that laced up at the side over a wheat-brown blouse, complete with lightweight but sturdy spaulders and bracers on her forearms. Her boots were well worn.

"Well," she said, getting to her feet, "I guess your going to try and kill me now, right?"

"I don't think I want to do that. I think we can help each other."

"And split the treasure?" she asked, aghast. "I told you: I don't plan on sharing."

"Good, I care not for coin."

Eviri seemed to be at a loss for words, her mouth opening and closing as she decided how to respond. "Then why are you looking for the crypt?"

"I have my own reasons. When we find the crypt you can claim the treasure for yourself, I swear it. Just don't slit my throat while I sleep." Bheren lay down on the ground and rested back against the same log he'd been sitting on earlier, hands clasped behind his head. "If you don't, then I can help you retrieve it."

"No promises," Eviri simmered as she sat down on the opposite side of the campfire and glowered at him. Despite her choleric disposition though, and her attempted assassination of him, Bheren felt that he was safe to assume she saw the advantages in his offer.

"How did you come to hear the name Bloodfire?" he asked, positioning himself more comfortably and grabbing his pack to use as a pillow.

"I heard it in Skell. There were rumors of a wandering man—a giant of a man—who could bend fire to his will and control it. Apparently a traveler saw you use it on a group of raiders up north. I had a hunch after seeing you up close."

Bheren recalled the event in question. It happened not so long ago on the shores of Soul Lake. He was ambushed and was forced to use his magic to escape with his life. It was unfortunate that he'd been seen, but he had no other choice at the time.

"You said a demon cursed you?" Eviri asked after a moment.

She received only the sound of gentle snoring in response and watched as the fiery light in Bheren's veins faded away.

*****

The next morning brought with it darkening skies and the scent of rain. Bheren had them packing up camp early and trekking south down the river. Based on the crude map he'd been given they'd want to nearly reach the lawless town of Mensil before turning east towards the region of Harratus. He didn't know exactly what to look for when they got there, but between the two of them he was sure they would manage.

Most of that morning was spent devoid of conversation or banter. It seemed like Eviri had yet to warm up to the idea of working with an accomplice. He was pondering how to spark up a conversation when the rain finally came, which put an end to such musings. The drops came heavy and pattered hard against the earth, soaking them from head to toe. Bheren let his molten blood boil up just enough so that the water evaporated off of him in a constant cloud of steam. He risked a glance back and saw Eviri glaring daggers at him from beneath a cowl that clung to her head like a wet rag.

He couldn't help but laugh, which was perhaps unwise. "You look like a drowned rat," he called back.

"You look like a knuckle-dragging clout," she returned snidely.

Bheren sighed heavily and gazed out to the farmer's fields, "The same rain that drowns the rat will grow the hay…" he mumbled.

Mensil was within sight before long; the rain had not subsided. The downpour was so intense that Bheren had given up trying to evaporate the water from his body. Having memorized the map so that he didn't have to pull it out, he began veering towards the craggy landscape beyond the fields. Eviri, however, seemed to have other ideas. She disregarded her companion entirely and continued straight towards the not-too-distant town.

"It's this way!" he called over the din of the rain.

"Good luck!" she replied without looking back. "I'll catch up with you when I'm dry and I've had a hot meal."

He cursed and pinched the bridge of his nose between his thumb and index finger. There was no obligation to go with her, *she* was the one who tried to attack *him*. If she didn't want to come with him, that was her choice. He looked to the Harratus region and back at Eviri's quickly receding form several times before growling something unintelligible and following the angry footprints left in the mud. It wouldn't hurt to eat something hardy and maybe even get some proper sleep. It had been some time since he'd slept on anything but the ground.

Bheren later found her, in dry clothes, sitting inside a tavern called The Wandering Blade. He made his way through the rough-and-tumble crowd to sit with her, drawing more attention than he cared for as he did.

"You found me," she smiled glibly.

"Well, there's only one tavern in town so I went out on a limb and assumed you might be here," he replied.

"Hello there," a barmaid approached their table with a bowl of what appeared to be rabbit stew and a glass of red wine. She set the items down before Eviri and turned to Bheren, "Can I get you anything?" The barmaid was rather attractive, he thought, with dark curls bouncing over the bare alabaster skin of her shoulders. She patiently awaited his reply, her hazel eyes sparkling in the firelight.

"I'll have the same," he said, gesturing to Eviri's meal.

The barmaid bobbed in a quick curtsey and disappeared into the crowd, promising a swift return.

"It's quiet tonight, relatively speaking," Eviri said when she was gone.

"You've been here before?"

She smirked, "Of course I have."

Bheren pointed to the wine and gave his companion an inquisitive look.

"Portshield Wine, from Wellhaven. It's dry, but it certainly has character."

He hadn't had wine from Wellhaven before, and although he preferred sweeter Udjatan wine he was willing to try it.

Bheren glanced around the tavern. All sorts of folk milled about, most engaged in raucous laughter. Each one of them, blades for hire, thieves, vagrants, adventurers, and merchants of illicit wares, found themselves in Mensil because society had tossed them out. Mensil had always been a place for those who had no home or anywhere else to go that wouldn't ostracize them. The Imperials left the town alone, for the most part, unless a wanted criminal was suspected to be hidden amongst the usual riffraff.

He noted the eyes of a hooded man studying them.

The barmaid returned with his meal, set it down before him with a captivating smile and spun to another table. The stew smelled wonderful. He sipped the wine and found it to be quite good, despite being on the drier side.

"I purchased two rooms for the night," Eviri said between bites. "We can set out early on the morrow."

Bheren looked up, truly surprised by the act of kindness, "My thanks," he said.

"Don't thank me yet, dinner is on you."

He grinned, "Fair." It was nice to see her warming up a little.

They had nearly finished their meal when their silent observer strode up to the table and stood before them. He was older than Eviri but not quite

Bheren's age. The man bore a longsword of Imperial make, likely stolen, strapped to his hip. Boiled leather armor with no insignia covered most of his body. Eviri, he noticed, couldn't stop staring at the scar that ran across the man's left eye.

"Can I help you?" Bheren asked.

"You two seem like quite the odd pair to be traveling together. I had thought she might be your daughter"—this drew a scowl form Eviri—"but you look nothing alike." The man's eyes kept drifting over to the bow and satchel of arrows slung over the back of Eviri's chair.

Eviri polished off her wine and set down her wooden goblet, "Why do you feel like it's any of your business?"

Bheren sighed, he found he'd been doing that a lot since meeting Eviri, "What's your name, friend?"

Ignoring Eviri's snide inquiry, the man turned his attention to Bheren, "My name is Orbin, from Heibi. I've been looking for a company to travel with. You two seem capable of handling yourselves. Would you have any interest in letting me join you for a few days?"

"As you said, Orbin," Eviri said before Bheren could reply, "we can handle ourselves."

Unsure of how to handle Bheren's feisty companion, Orbin looked to the large man for an answer. "Why do you want to come with us?" Bheren asked. "You don't even know where we're going."

"Your destination matters not to me, and my reasons are my own. I swear to you I mean you no harm. My blade is yours for as long as I'm with you. These roads have become dangerous, and I can help you fight. If need be."

Bheren considered him for a long moment before inviting him to sit down, paying no mind to the look of horror that washed over Eviri's face as he did. Orbin didn't strike him as dangerous, and he sounded genuine enough, but looks could be deceiving. He would be keeping a close eye on him. The barmaid, seeing that another had joined them, flitted back over to offer refreshments. Orbin ordered a pint but nothing more. They spoke for a while, ruminating about the goings-on of the world and getting a feel for each other, until, just before midnight, the tavern bar closed and they were forced to retire for the night.

"You know he's running from the empire," Eviri said upstairs as she opened the door to her modestly furnished lodgings.

"Yes," he replied, "I suspected as much."

"So, why did you agree to take him with us? You remember, I hope, that I'm not interested in sharing the loot."

Bheren shrugged, "I trusted you didn't I? I still don't know very much about you either, but I was willing to give you a chance. You might have killed me the night we met, as I slept, but instead you dragged me to Mensil and bought me a warm bed for the night. Besides, Orbin isn't wrong about the roads being dangerous these days."

Eviri furrowed her brow and narrowed her eyes, "I

hardly dragged you here."

"Goodnight Eviri," he chuckled, turning to continue to his own room. Behind him he heard the slightly agitated closing of her door and smiled.

*****

Bheren was up well before any of them, he sat on the porch of The Wandering Blade and considered the previous couple of days. He certainly hadn't planned on taking a group to the crypt with him but, having strength in numbers didn't hurt any.

"You're up early," said Eviri, coming to stand behind him.

He craned his neck around to see her already armed and ready to go, "I guess I'm just anxious to set out," he said.

"You don't strike me as the anxious type." She moved to sit down with him on the steps, "I hope we can trust Orbin."

Bheren put a hand on her shoulder, "Trust *me*."

Eviri looked down at his hand like a frightened deer ready to flee, but just as quickly he saw her relax. He felt like he needed to be very tactful with the woman, she seemed to trust nobody and assumed the worst of everyone. To a certain extent, he thought to himself, that wasn't a bad thing, but she also needed to allow herself to make friends — friends that would help her walk the dangerous roads and face the perils of Helsyndel with her.

"I hope you haven't been waiting long." They both turned to see Orbin standing in the doorway.

"*Hours*, Orbin," came Eviri's sharp, if satiric, reply, "we've been waiting for hours."

Bheren rolled his eyes, "Not quite," and to Orbin he said, "regardless, we are ready to depart."

"I'd like to show you something before we go," he said. With a brief hesitation he stepped aside. Behind him stood a young woman with wheat-blond hair that hung down either side of her head in long braids, coming to rest on her delicate shoulders. She wore no armor. Instead, she had donned simple travel clothes with a woolen shawl draped over her shoulders.

She looked quite nervous.

"Well met," the woman said timidly.

"This is my sister," Orbin urged her to take a step forward. "Her name is Mia."

Eviri leveled an expressionless, yet somehow scathing, look at Bheren, who was at a loss for words. "Where we are going is no place for a-" he was about to say child but thought better of it. "She will be in danger," he said instead.

"Mia can help us," Orbin countered, "she's a healer."

"I studied under Mei Si, the Ocoyan healer," said Mia. "I can be useful, I promise."

Bheren had not yet divulged to their new acquaintance where they were going or what they were doing, but now, concerned for Mia's well-being, he decided to do so. "We are looking for a crypt around Harratus rumored to be full of treasure. I fear for Mia's safety should we run into trouble — and I suspect we may."

The mention of treasure seemed not to have provoked a reaction.

"We don't need to follow you that far," pressed Orbin. "We'll accompany you only until the region's border and part ways."

Somehow Bheren suspected that wouldn't be the case. Regardless, he stood, casting a scrutinizing eye at Mia, and began walking towards the west edge of town without a word. Eviri followed him, clearly not enthused by the turn of events.

Orbin looked to Mia, "I guess we should follow."

His sister nodded her agreement and they hurried after the pair.

Bheren hadn't told them yet about his Bloodfire and he intended to keep it that way, for now — it was clear that they hadn't recognized him as Eviri had. It was his greatest weapon and had saved his life many times over. Perhaps it would become necessary to divulge his secret, but at the moment he saw no advantage in telling them.

The skies were mostly clear, unlike the day before, though everything was still wet from the rain and the smell of damp earth hung like mist in the air. The road seemed quiet; the party saw no other signs of activity other than a small caravan heading into Mensil. Usually there were scores of folks crossing the Red River from Kaleia to Lersal and back, but he supposed they were still too far south on the road to see any of that traffic.

Around noon Bheren veered them off the path and into the fields, careful to not disturb the crops too much. Fields gave way to a harsher, rockier landscape and after a while the air became noticeably warmer. After another hour of navigating the unforgiving terrain they crested a large hill and were able to see the volcanic mountain Harratus in the distance.

Mia gazed out to the great mountain with a mix of unease and awe. It seemed to Bheren like she hadn't seen much of eastern Illthashore, and the mountain was certainly an imposing spectacle.

"The crypt should be somewhere down in that gorge," Bheren said, checking his map and gesturing to the multitudes of giant rock formations and boulders below. He turned to Orbin, "This would be a good time to part ways."

Orbin was about to reply when a javelin whisked by them. Bheren thought it missed its mark until he followed the javelin's trajectory and saw Eviri on the ground with the weapon protruding from her lower abdomen. Another grazed past his arm, leaving an angry gash along his bicep. He instinctively allowed his Bloodfire to boil to the surface as Mia streaked past them to tend to Eviri. Orbin's eyes went wide and he swore as Bheren became a living torch beside him. Having more pressing matters to attend to though, he drew his sword and turned towards the directions the projectiles came from.

Cresting the hillock behind them were three ruddy little creatures standing only as tall as Bheren's waist. He recognized them as Kobolds, a biped reptilian race native to southern Illthashore. They wore patchwork armor and had thick cowls drawn up over their heads to protect them from the sun. Kobolds didn't like the sun.

This must only be a scouting party, he thought, usually they would attack in larger tribal war bands. Bheren roared at the little monsters and rushed towards them. The third Kobold threw its own javelin at him but he dodged it mid-sprint. The other two drew knives from beneath their rags. Bheren slammed into one of the knife-wielding Kobolds with the force of a battering ram and lifted it off its feet. The creature immediately began thrashing and stabbing and screeching. Holding it in a bear-hug, he unleashed his inner fire and reduced it to a pile of ash.

Bheren knew he'd been stabbed multiple times, but he didn't let that slow him as he spun to see Orbin engaged with the other two. The Kobolds were trying to flank him, fortunately the man was too quick and was always able to stay one step ahead of them. One of the Kobolds lunged at him. Orbin rushed forward to meet the creature, who wasn't expecting such a brazen retort. The Kobold tried to backpedal but was too late to avoid Orbin's slashing blade—which took its head clean off.

The last Kobold, seeing one of its companions beheaded and the other turned to ash, tried to flee. Bheren was about to give chase when an arrow flew past him and struck the retreating Kobold in the back, sending it sprawling to the ground. He looked back to see Eviri standing, the bloody javelin on the ground beside her, and holding her bow. Mia stood next to her.

It was over quickly, the whole encounter seeming like a blur. "Eviri," Bheren strode up to her, allowing the Bloodfire to fade and trying to ignore the pain where the Kobold's knife had cut deep. She grimaced by way of greeting, still hurting but otherwise faring well considering how severely she'd been injured.

"They didn't stand a chance," she said, never

lacking confidence.

Mia took the opportunity to assess Bheren's injuries, it seemed like she either hadn't seen him use his Bloodfire or didn't care. "Hold still," she bade him. The young woman held her hand over his arm and spoke words of a language he didn't recognize. Waves of comforting warmth washed over him. He could feel the gash closing beneath Mia's palm. She did the same for his stab wounds. Even the fatigue he felt from unleashing his Bloodfire had vanished.

"Mei Si, you said?" he asked Mia, studying his unmarred arm.

She smiled coyly, "Yes, she was a good teacher."

"Eviri will need to rest," Mia continued. "I've done what I can for now, but I'll need to do more healing as she sleeps. The body heals naturally when we sleep, my magic is strongest when it can assist that process."

"We should make camp down in the valley, we're too exposed up here," Orbin suggested, appearing next to them but making sure to stand a couple arm lengths away from Bheren. "There is no doubt more of them wandering the hills. We need to make ourselves scarce."

Eviri winced as she took a step forward, "Couldn't have put it better myself," she said, accepting the use of Mia's shoulder to lean on.

"You three go," Bheren said. "These bodies need to be burned or the smell will bring them straight here." Orbin nodded in agreement, obvious questions lingering in the air between them, and began leading the two women down into the valley. Bheren noticed the man glance back at the ashes that were once a Kobold with a wary eye.

He turned to the remaining bodies of their attackers when they were gone, letting the Bloodfire simmer to the surface again.

Perhaps keeping those two around wouldn't be such a bad idea after all.

*****

Later that night Bheren and Orbin sat around a fire concealed in a small cave. Eviri lay on the ground not far away, within the radius of light shed by the blaze and sleeping soundly. Mia hovered beside her in an almost trance-like state, murmuring softly to herself in the same language she'd spoken earlier that day.

"What tongue is that?" Bheren asked Mia's brother.

Orbin glanced over to the women, "It's a language from the Bessekai region in Ocoya, taught to her by Mei Si."

"Has Mia ever been to the Bessekai region?"

Orbin chuckled softly, "She's never been to Ocoya, never mind *that* part of the province. From what little I've heard of it, Bessekai is a place most folks wouldn't survive unless they're skilled in the arcane arts. Mia tells me it's a place that only the Madou Shi can go — Ocoyan mages."

Bheren listened attentively, the mysterious land far to the north fascinated him a great deal. The discovery of Ocoya was still fairly recent in

Helsyndel's history. Trade between the two provinces had been established but the Ocoyans hadn't, at least so far, been open to the idea of regular visitations from Helsyndillians.

The fire spit and crackled.

"She wants to go there one day," Orbin added, "Mia really admired Mei Si."

"What happened to her?" Bheren asked. "To Mei Si."

"She had to return home," replied Orbin, a flicker of bitterness in his tone. "Family business, Mia said. Ocoyan's have strong family ties, ancestry is extremely important to them. Their kin come before everything, apparently."

"As it should," said Bheren.

Orbin shrugged watching another ember take flight, "Maybe. But she could have at least done more to make sure Mia was comfortable before she left her like that."

Bheren regarded the man, his expression becoming serious, "I think it's time you told me why you and your sister are traveling with us."

"Only if you tell me how you were able to burn up that Kobold," said Orbin, looking up from the fire.

Bheren held his gaze, pondering how to go about telling his tale. "A demon cursed me as a child after it killed my parents and brother," he began. "It attacked us in the night. I know not where it came from, or why it chose to spare me. My blood has possessed a searing fire ever since that day. I've learned to control it — and to live with the pain — but there was a time that it boiled to the surface without warning. It was a rough time in my life. There were times..." he hesitated, "there were times I gave up hope and tried to end my suffering. Obviously I failed.

And so, until I was able to harness it, I lived in the wilds north of Greyelo. After I'd mastered my affliction I returned to civilization and settled in Skell. I worked there as a blacksmith until fate summoned me, and now I am here."

"Searing fire? How can you endure the pain of that

pumping through your veins?"

"When I bring it to the surface it's agonizing, but in my solitude I learned to fight through it. Now, when the fire is at rest, it's merely an annoyance."

"Has it done your body any lasting damage?"

"No," Bheren replied. "On the contrary the heat has staved off disease and can warm me on the coldest of winter nights. Sicknesses cannot abide to take root in me. Demons are cruel, and this one wished for me to live long and suffer."

Orbin stared into the flames, lost in thought.

Bheren tossed a log onto the fire, shattering his reverie. "Your turn," he said.

"Mia and I are orphans as well," he began, "our mother died when we were young. Mia never knew our father. He left us after mother passed. I took care of us until Mei Si found us and took Mia under her wing as a healer. Mei Si offered to teach me as well, but I was content living as a street urchin."

Bheren raised an eyebrow as if to ask why.

Orbin lifted a shoulder and let it fall, "It was not

my path, and I was working my way into some profitable dealings."

"I visited my sister from time to time," he continued, "but, as I grew older, business took me away from her. Eventually I learned that Mei Si had gone back to Ocoya, like I said, leaving Mia to fend for herself. I returned home to Heibi to find Mia at an orphanage. By that time though I'd run into some trouble with the imperials and had to travel cautiously.

I took her away with me. We spent a year on Pirate's Rock—which was quite the experience—then another handful of years in Asperia, where imperial rule isn't as strong. But, circumstance eventually drove us away from Asperia. We traveled across Hymult, where I was forced to kill an imperial after we happened across a patrol." Orbin cast a sidelong glance at the sword resting against the log beside him. "We managed to escape, making our way to the Greywood. We've been on the run ever since."

Bheren was silent for a long time. Finally, he spoke, "And you're traveling with us to avoid notice. You needed a way to discreetly get away from legion controlled territory across the river, and the imperials aren't looking for a group."

Orbin's silence confirmed Bheren's musings.

"Why us?" the big man asked.

"You and Eviri looked capable and..."

"...trusting?" Bheren finished for him. "There were plenty of other capable warriors in that tavern."

"Call it instinct," said Orbin.

Bheren looked over to check on Eviri and Mia, not much had changed. "You thought she would be safer with you, on the run, than at the orphanage?"

"I couldn't leave her there," was all he got in response. It was all he needed, he understood.

Bheren surmised that Mia had honed her skills as a healer as she and her brother traversed Helsyndel. He had seen other healers in his own travels, and most of them couldn't hold a candle to Mia.

"We'll leave in the morning," said Orbin. "I told

you we would part ways before you reached the crypt."

"That won't be necessary," Bheren replied. "You can come with us, if that is what you want."

Orbin considered the offer but seemed to be struggling with an unspoken question.

"Eviri will share in the riches, probably," he said, checking quickly to see if somehow she had heard him. All was quiet. "I'm sure we can convince her to part with some of it. You can buy Mia and yourself protection and passage to another continent. Alland, I imagine, would be a good choice. The Empire holds no sway there."

"What is *your* reason for doing this?" Orbin asked. "You seem to have no interest in the spoils, or so I've gathered."

Bheren remained silent.

"Alright then, keep your secrets."

The rest of the night passed without trouble. When Mia finished her healing spell she fell into a deep slumber next to Eviri while Orbin and Bheren took turns keeping watch.

Tomorrow they would reach their destination.

*****

The sun had risen nearly to its apex by the time they stumbled upon the crypt the next day. They had trekked south from their campsite after a meager breakfast, following Bheren's map as best as they were able.

Eviri seemed much better. There was a slight scar to the lower right of her navel but otherwise the wound was only a painful memory. She was having no trouble keeping pace and her generally cynical disposition had softened considerably. Bheren knew she was just thankful to be alive. For all her sarcasm and acerbity, Eviri was truly a good soul. Under that hard exterior was a compassionate heart.

Bheren spoke briefly with her about the conversation he'd had with Orbin the previous night and, with grudging acceptance, she ceded to his argument that their companions should be allowed to share in a small portion of the wealth, if only so that they could eke out a better life for themselves.

The crypt's entrance was as nondescript as Bheren expected it to be. Mia was the first to see it, nestled in amongst a cairn of large boulders that were built around it to disguise its heavy stone door. The door was already cracked open just enough for a grown man to squeeze through—left that way by previous grave robbers who never returned from the cold darkness beyond. Bheren felt the hairs on his arms rise as a shudder swept through him. The others must have felt it too, it was as it a pall of dread had fallen over them. He could see it in their eyes as he glanced back at them.

Ancient text adorned the masonry surrounding the crypt but none of them were able to read it. It was likely that there were few, if any, who could. No statues or religious effigies marked the significance of the sepulcher. Its only adornment were two columns that held up a stone slab above the doorway, creating an archway of sorts. The crypt's entrance radiated a spine-chilling air that filled Bheren with unease.

Eviri looked at Bheren, "Well, this was your idea. Lead the way."

Bheren offered her a dubious sidelong glance. "Is everyone ready?" he asked.

"As ready as we'll ever be I suppose," said Orbin. Mia nodded, though she looked several shades paler. The pair walked up to stand with the others, all of them transfixed by the darkness beyond the door.

Bheren took one of the torches lashed to his pack, lit it, and proceeded into the crypt. The others followed. The air inside was dry and cool. Bheren led them down a small flight of stairs to a hallway which they followed for what felt like longer than it probably was. The budding sense of dread that they all felt on the surface grew as they delved farther into the shadowy depths.

None of them dared to speak until they came to what seemed to be the crypt's central chamber. The torchlight revealed six old wooden caskets resting on stone slabs, three on each side of them, lining the walls of the chamber. At the far side of the room was a raised sarcophagus adorned with more runic script similar to what they'd seen outside. The lid of the sarcophagus rested askew, adding to the trepidation they all felt. Bheren stopped and listened to the intense silence. Their own breathing and the faint crackling of the torch seemed deafening in this place.

Orbin forged ahead and used the tip of his sword to lift the lid of one of the caskets. The contents took their breath away. It was filled to the brim with gold coins that glittered in the light of the torch. Eviri failed to contain a little squeal of delight and skipped up to Orbin. She whistled softly, estimating the value held in the casket, and reached out to pick up a coin.

Her fingers passed right through the coins,

grasping nothing but stale air. She tried again with the same result. She strode up the next casket and, after removing the lid to find more coins, tried to pick those up too. No luck. Her hands came up empty; frustration was clear in her expression.

Hollow, rasping laughter filled the chamber.

Bheren's blood ran cold—if such a thing were possible.

"I call it fools gold," said a coarse voice from somewhere in the darkness beyond the sarcophagus. "For only fools come to seek it."

Eviri knocked an arrow and Orbin hefted his sword, but Bheren knew that neither weapon would do them much good.

From the shadows emerged a tall humanoid form. Dark plate armor covered its muscular body. The creature stared at them with ophidian eyes, sizing up its next victims with every step it took. It's ruddy skin was dry, cracked and bleeding, but it didn't seem bothered by it.

It grinned at them through rows of serrated teeth,

"It has been a long time since I've had the pleasure of company. My name is Balmonek."

"*Foul demon*," spat Orbin.

Balmonek chuckled, "Bold words, Orbin of Heibi."

Orbin sucked in a breath, "How do you know my name?"

"I know all of you," Balmonek rasped, glaring at each of them in turn. His eyes lingered on Eviri before coming to rest on Bheren, "Hello, *Bloodfire*."

All eyes turned to Bheren, who remained silent.

"You know this thing?" Eviri asked incredulously.

Bheren nodded, "This is the demon that cursed me."

Eviri's eyes widened as realization dawned on her, "You knew the demon was going to be here? And you led us here anyway?"

Bheren shook his head, "I did not know, not for sure, but I had my suspicions. And would you have rather come here alone, like you originally intended?"

"Could have at least warned us," she muttered,

letting the matter drop.

"I imagine you are here to try and kill me," said Balmonek, speaking to Bheren. "I'm surprised that it took you so long to find me, *Bloodfire*. I see you've learned to control the fire coursing through your veins."

"I've learned enough to be able to send you back to the Void," he gritted.

The demon's hollow laughter filled the crypt once more, "I don't doubt you will try. Come, then. Let's see how you have learned to use my gift."

Bheren wasted no time letting his Bloodfire rise to the surface, once again becoming a human torch and rushing the demon with fury born of seething hatred. In a heartbeat he had covered the distance between them and threw a punch at the one who cursed him. Sparks and motes of flame showered the stone floor as Bheren's fiery fist connected with the demon's jaw and a loud crack echoed through the chamber. He followed it up with a head-butt that sent the demon stumbling backwards.

Balmonek made a noise that sounded like a coughing wheeze, which Bheren realized was just laughter distorted by a broken jaw. The demon reached up, grasped its chin, and snapped its lower jaw back into place. "Is that all?"

Bheren roared and charged again. This time Balmonek met Bheren's assault with a vicious kick that struck him mid-chest and sent him flying back to land at the feet of his companions.

Now that Eviri had a clear shot she loosed an arrow at the demon. Balmonek caught the projectile with one hand, snapped it, and let go a torrent of purple flames at the party. Eviri dove behind one of the caskets as Mia cast a spell over herself and her brother, allowing the flames to wash over them harmlessly. Bheren took the full brunt of the attack but seemed resistant to the conflagration. Eviri shot the demon again from behind cover but this time the arrow simply bounced off its plate armor.

Orbin, after making sure Mia was alright, produced three throwing knives from his belt. He sent all of them whizzing towards the demon in rapid succession. One of the knives skipped off its armor, another grazed its ear, and the last buried itself into the demon's unprotected forearm. Balmonek seemed unperturbed by the embedded knife, he yanked it out and tossed it aside to clatter on the stone.

Mia cast another spell, this time targeting Bheren, granting him renewed stamina as he once again threw himself at Balmonek. The demon's eyes began glowing with an eerie violet light. Bheren was able to land another punch before he was thrown backwards again, this time nearly taking out Orbin in the process.

Balmonek narrowly avoided another arrow and turned his attention to Eviri. He held out a hand towards her, "Sleep," he commanded. Eviri did just that. She swayed first, trying to resist the magic, and then collapsed onto the floor. Mia rushed over to her and immediately set to work casting a cantrip to combat the cursed slumber.

With the two women out of the way Balmonek was able to focus solely on the two men. Unfortunately for him, the curse he'd cast on Eviri distracted him just long enough for Orbin to toss more knives, one of which implanted itself into his right eye as he turned to face them. Balmonek screeched, ripping out the projectile in a gush of crimson blood and clasping his hands over the grievous wound.

Bheren closed in for a third time and grasped the demon's head in both hands. His arms began glowing like molten rock as he concentrated as much of the Bloodfire as he could into his arms and out through his palms. Balmonek wailed, matching Bheren's own roar of anguish, as searing waves of heat radiated into his temples. The demon began emitting purple fire across his whole body just before Bheren was thrown backwards for the third time, this time with much more force, as Balmonek erupted in an intense wave of demon-fire. Bheren hit the far wall and crumpled to the floor, dazed.

The demon stood, alive but far from unharmed.

Wisps of smoke rose from his armor and a steady stream flowed from the eye socket Orbin punctured with the throwing knife. The smoke pouring from his right eye became thick and oily. When it cleared the eye had returned to normal. Balmonek stalked towards them, still radiating enough heat to singe the stone he walked upon.

Bheren propped himself up to his elbows and glanced over at Eviri, whose eyes were fluttering open thanks to Mia. She looked back to him with evident confusion. They held the gaze for several heartbeats. Bheren knew that she would understand what he needed her to do. He mouthed the words *"get them out."* Eviri's confused expression became one of alarm as Bheren stood and strode with purpose towards Balmonek. He and the demon locked eyes long enough to know that whatever happened next would spell the end for one of them.

"Balmonek," Bheren raised a hand to the infernal demon, "burn." Fire roared from Bheren's palm. Balmonek responded in kind. The temperature in the room became instantly unbearable. Eviri, Mia and Orbin coughed and choked as they grouped together and made for the exit. Eviri risked one last glance back towards Bheren, who had become a pillar of fire as bright as the sun, and ran from the crypt.

The caskets burned to ash, the illusions within fading, and the stone slabs they rested on began melting and bubbling. Bheren roared at the demon and let his Bloodfire pour out of him, allowing his anger to eclipse the mind-numbing pain wracking his body. The demon-fire that Balmonek was contesting him with was strong, but it wasn't enough to hold back the fury of Bheren's blistering assault. The stream of Bheren's flames gradually pushed back the purple fires of the demon until Balmonek, looking shocked and panicked, was overwhelmed.

Another wail, this one desperate and guttural, filled the blazing crypt. Bheren continued unleashing Bloodfire, having reached the point of no return and unable to stop himself. He let his inner fire loose until not even the sarcophagus behind where Balmonek stood remained.

Agony ripped through him, but at least Balmonek was no more. The Bloodfire, the demon's own curse, had incinerated Balmonek as soon as it swept over him, leaving not even the plate armor behind. Bheren threw his head back and cried out in pain.

Darkness overcame him.

*****

Eviri went back down into the crypt when she was able to. It had to have been an hour before she was even able to descend the stairs leading into the darkness below, and even when she did the stone around her was still uncomfortably warm.

No sign of Bheren or the demon remained. It appeared as if they had both burnt up in the inferno. Eviri knelt where Bheren had stood in his final moment, indicated by a scorch mark, and placed her hand on the floor. After a moment of silent rumination she stood, thanking Bheren for saving them, and left the crypt without looking back.

*****

The trio traveled north along the road after a night of much needed rest back in Mensil. Before reaching Lersal they veered to the east, making their way north of the Arcaneus and along Illthashore's eastern coast up to Greyelo. Here they shared one more meal and toasted in honor of their fallen comrade before parting ways the next morning.

Orbin and Mia would continue traveling along the coast towards Pinnacle in the far north. The journey was a dangerous one, but Eviri had confidence in their ability to handle themselves.

Eviri herself would head west, past the Shrine of Mal'ethiel, on the road to Skell. Here she would need to decide her next course of action. Having been cheated out of the crypt's reputed treasure was truly unfortunate, and so she would need to find an alternative means of procuring coin.

Shouldn't be too hard, she thought, Helsyndel was a big place.

*****

Bheren opened his eyes, groaned, and pushed himself up to a sitting position. He was laying in a craggy field that appeared similar to the landscape around Harratus, but here the skies were a roiling red mass of thick clouds and the horizon rippled like a mirage in every direction. Perhaps Harratus had erupted? The last thing he remembered was watching the demon Balmonek burn to nothingness. After that his memory was a haze of incredibly bright light and pain.

Then he was here.

"How do you fare, warrior?"

Bheren searched for the disembodied voice

echoing around him.

"You are in the elemental plane of fire."

The shape of a woman began forming from the shimmering heat in the distance. Her image became clearer as she drew near. Long fiery locks spilled down her back and tiny flames flickered to life with every step she took, vanishing once her bare feet left the rock. At first it looked like she wore nothing, but Bheren quickly realized that wasn't the case. The woman wore a form-fitting dress wreathed in indolent flame. It was difficult to tell whether it was her garment that was ablaze or if her body was made entirely of fire.

"My name is Fleryah," she said to him as he stood to greet her. "I am the embodiment of the element of fire in Helsyndel."

Bheren affected a smile, still very much perplexed, "My name is Bheren, I'm-"

"Dead," she finished for him. "Your physical body burned up in that extraordinary display against the demon Balmonek. Impressive work."

Bheren stammered, unsure what to say or how to react. "How do you know that?" he asked after finding his voice.

Fleryah held out a hand and a globe of fire formed in her palm. Within the globe Bheren saw men and women rushing around with buckets of water, throwing the contents on a thatched cruck that was nothing less than a raging fireball. "I can scry through fire anywhere in Illthashore, and sometimes beyond if the blaze is large enough. *You*, Bheren, most certainly caught my attention in that Harratian crypt. You have a gift, but your control over it is juvenile. Let me teach you to become something truly spectacular."

Bheren's eyes darted between Fleryah and the globe, "You wish for me to become one of your disciples?"

The fiery woman nodded, "If that is what you wish, Bheren. I can train you here in my realm, and when you are ready you will be reborn to the world of the living like a phoenix rising from the ashes.

You will retain your memories, of course."

"If I refuse?" He already knew what he wanted, but curiosity got the better of him.

Her demeanor grew solemn, "Then you will leave this place and continue on your way to the afterlife."

Bheren exhaled. He wasn't overly surprised that he died, but it was still a lot to process, "I will stay here," he declared.

Fleryah's radiant smile touched her ears, "Then I am pleased, and you will not be disappointed."

He thought about being resurrected and found himself contemplating whether or not he would be able to find Eviri or Orbin and Mia when he was. Eviri in particular had struck a chord in him, even though their time together had been brief. The more he thought about it, however, the more he realized the unlikelihood of that ever happening. They would have grown old by the time he was born again.

Fleryah came to stand close enough for him to see the fires of her realm dancing in her eyes.

"Let us begin."

Saeculum Secunda

Nayeli Ackart ran from her room to the moonlit balcony, heart racing, not even bothering to cover herself. She'd been woken by a violent tremor that rumbled through the Ackart manse and the city of Ashport beyond. By the sound of the shouts drifting over the early morning breeze, she wasn't the only one that had been roused by the quake.

She shivered uncontrollably and hugged herself tight, feeling the prickle of goosebumps across her skin. Spring had yet to relinquish its hold on Alland and its chill lingered on the air.

Voices from within the manse brought her back to the moment. Nayeli strode back in and hurriedly threw on a nightgown just before her door burst open and Orson Ackart, her father, nearly stumbled in. He breathed a sigh of relief when he saw his daughter—his only child.

"Father, what was that?"

Orson, a handsome man for his age with his

graying hair and regal poise, took his daughter's hand and lead her out of the room. "We must leave Ashport, *now*! Your mother is already waiting in the courtyard."

"What's going on? Can't I at least get properly changed?"

Her father didn't answer, he didn't even slow his frantic pace. "The Viridian Isles have been destroyed, and we're next in its path."

Nayeli shook her head in disbelief, making her blond curls bounce, scared and confused. "What? The Isles are gone!?"

Orson didn't speak again until they were sitting in the carriage with her mother, Mallory, who appeared to be in no better a state than she was. This must be serious, she thought, if her mother hadn't even taken the time to appear prim and proper.

"Father," she said, determined not to be brushed off again, "what's going on!?"

Orson rapped on the carriage wall and they took

off at a trot. "Something happened on the Isles," he began. "According to my sources, an ancient life form was awakened there late last night. A Primordial. The Primordial razed Argishill and moved east out to sea. I don't know exactly what happened, but it's heading towards Ashport."

Nayeli was about to ask what a Primordial was when an ear-splitting thunderclap shook the city. A bolt of lightning struck the city's bell tower, reducing it to dust and blackened stone in an instant. The residual arcs, and there were many, similarly erased several other buildings from the cityscape, including the Ackart manse. Nayeli and her parents, had they stayed for even a moment longer, would have been reduced to rubble!

The horses spooked and jerked to the right, causing the carriage to swerve jarringly.

Nayeli thought back to her studies at the Academia Nobilis in Gispia. It was there that she learned of the nightmarish creatures that stalked Helsyndel, and other horrors of bygone ages, but never had she heard of a being such as this. This being that had just laid waste to the city she grew up in, to her home, and to the life she knew.

"We have to make for Alland Rock," said her father, "Your mother and I know a Priestess of Keagaia there who may be able to help. Those devout to the elements are better attuned to these things."

Nayeli glanced back at their home, or lack thereof, feeling tears welling up in her eyes. She had friends in Ashport. Friends she would never see again. Friends that by morning would be crushed beneath the ruins of a city. She thought off all the people who wouldn't make it out in time, and of the Isles, swept into the history books overnight.

And she wept.

To be continued...

The Halls

of Amenti

"Our perception of the world only goes so far as our senses can understand it, beyond that is open to conjecture. I wonder if we have been given a gift in not being able to see beyond our narrow scope of reality."

- Nathan Challis

The Halls of Amenti

Back in the world we know...

Then for a dwelling place, far 'neath the earth crust,
blasted great spaces they by their power,
spaces apart from the children of men.
Surrounded them by forces and power,
shielded from harm they the Halls of the Dead.

- The Emerald Tablets of Thoth — B.C.E

I was once told by a friend that the desert was a terrible, unforgiving place. He wasn't wrong.

In the end though my pride as a fortune hunter overcame me. I had come into possession of a map supposedly leading to a treasure of incalculable wealth, buried beneath uncharted ruins somewhere in the vast Libyan desert, south of Benghazi. This was a once in a lifetime opportunity I couldn't pass up.

Elaine, my tenuous partner of many years, is the one who gave me the map during what was to be our final meeting. I'd rather not explain our circumstances at the time, but suffice it to say we are no longer a couple. She had been meaning to give it to me and I'm glad she did before we parted ways that day. Perhaps she did it out of spite, knowing that I wouldn't be able to resist temptation.

My friends told me to stick to trophy hunting in Africa, but my mind was made up. Many considered my expedition to be a fool's errand; I didn't care. Whatever their reasons, they wouldn't help me. I was on my own. At least I would get to prove them wrong and keep the riches for myself.

I spent many nights researching lore on this long-forgotten hoard, often finding nothing despite my efforts. That is until the fateful night I read an entry in a dead explorer's journal, acquired through somewhat illicit means, re-counting the astounding find. This though didn't go into any great detail, and of course I wasn't able to speak with the man, but at least I now had tangible proof of the treasure's existence.

Months after I was given the map would mark the day I left my home in Arkansas for Benghazi and, with my hired Arab entourage, traveled into the desert in search of the cache. Abd Al-Aziz, a shrewd Libyan man, was my native chaperone, and the only soul that knew of my true intent in the desert. Of course, he wanted a share of the profit as well as the small fortune I had already paid him.

I reluctantly agreed.

Two weeks we traveled the endless Cyrenaican sands until, weary and on the cusp of defeat, we saw it. There was no official name for the ruins, nor any official historical texts denoting their existence to tell of, and so Abd Al-Aziz dubbed the place *al-Maghrib*, meaning "the place of the sunset". The name he chose was fitting, I thought, as the first time we saw the ruins the sun was sinking down behind them, casting the old stone structures in the dying light of day. We made camp there that night, amongst the crumbling stone of a place lost to time.

I spent the late hours of that night gazing at the

stars while Abd Al-Aziz and the others laughed and joked amongst themselves. Visions of what we may find on the morrow filled my thoughts. I dreamt of fame and power, wealth and women, all of the things my exploits would bring me.

I woke to Abd Al-Aziz tapping my boot and repeating my name. "Dawson, Dawson Bradshaw", he said over and over. I sat up to find our entourage either packing up camp or perusing the ancient structures. More unpleasantly incessant prompting from my guide spurred me to wakefulness.

I had joined them in the search, but for what I wasn't sure. We spent many hours of that day studying every aspect of the Cyrenaican ruins. It wasn't until shortly after mid-day that we made some well-deserved progress.

Initially we thought what we'd stumbled upon was dry quicksand, but quicksand doesn't leave a gaping hole in the ground. The pit was found at the expense of one of Abd Al-Aziz's compatriots, who barely had time to scream before the earth swallowed him whole. I peered down into the bottomless chasm. The stale, musty air turned my stomach.

I've seen things that would drain the color from any ordinary man, but even I had to collect myself before further analysis of the geologic sinkhole. It was wide, wider than a man was tall. I suggested that the hired hands be lowered down first but they obstinately refused. Eventually I had to relent and volunteer as the first to be lowered into the pit. Abd Al-Aziz offered to go with me, at least, and after his fellow countrymen saw that he was willing to go, they did too. A few of the men naturally had to stay up top with the camels and supplies — they were the more superstitious bunch anyway.

The ropes used to lower us were old and frayed in places and I was relieved when my boots touched solid ground. The rays of sunlight shining down from above lit the area around us but nothing more. The man who had fallen was killed on impact, the back of his skull caved in on the cool stone. Torches were tossed down so that they could light our way. I led, holding the burning brand out before me and proceeding cautiously through the dank subterranean halls.

The winding maze of corridors led us through twisting passages and narrow channels that allowed only enough room to traverse single file. One such channel was particularly challenging. Abd Al-Aziz and I made it through unscathed, but when he called back for the others to proceed he was answered only with silence. He called out again but received nothing back save for the echo of his own voice. It seemed that our entourage had finally lost what shred of courage had compelled them to follow us into this wretched place.

We pressed on after a time but were stopped by a blood-curdling scream that echoed through the dark halls behind us. I froze, not knowing what to make of it at first. Abd Al-Aziz looked as dumbfounded as I. The outburst was followed by an eerie silence that lasted uncomfortably long.

For another hour or so we traversed the ageless subterranean realm. I began to think we would never find the riches we sought, until finally we came across a staircase descending into the bowels of *Duat* itself. Abd Al-Aziz, my stalwart guide, offered to lead, but I declined. What kind of fortune hunter would I be if I couldn't brave the underworld myself! He may have noticed my hesitation, but only because, for the briefest instant, I was sure I saw the eyes of a pale, sunken figure leering at us from the black abyss below. The light of my torch quickly quelled such phantasms of the imagination, though I couldn't help but feel as if our presence was unwelcome.

It was cold at the bottom, cold enough that I could see a cone of vapor exuded by my breath. Abd Al-Aziz was affected too, the man shivered and wrapped his headscarf tighter around his neck. I was transfixed by the age-old murals and time-worn texts adorning the walls. The light cast by my torch was bright enough to illuminate the bizarre hieroglyphs well enough for me to see every intricate detail, perfectly preserved by the darkness of untold thousands of years.

A door at the end of the long hall marked the way to what I was now sure to be the great lost treasure of *al-Maghrib*. I excitedly ran my fingers along the glyphs arrayed across the stone, trying to decipher their meaning.

After several minutes of this my hands brushed across a section of stone outlined by a barely discernible groove. I pressed my weight onto the stone, which yielded to the pressure and sank inward. There were the dull and distant thuds of shifting mortar before the heavy door shuddered for the first time in many millennia, sending billows of dust into the stagnant air. The entire slab of stone descended into the floor, leaving my Libyan friend and I coughing and squinting into the gloom.

Beyond was a chamber so gigantic it defied belief, I could scarcely fathom how such an immense space beneath the earth had not yet been discovered. Ten widely spaced columns, oddly Egyptian in design, towered into the darkness above to support a ceiling the meager light of our torches couldn't reach. The stone floor of the chamber was littered with scrolls from an unknown age, priceless artifacts, and ornate weaponry inlaid with precious gems. There were no heaping piles of gold coins and bejeweled goblets one might expect from the tales of fantasy novels, where greedy red dragons guarded their mountainous hoards of treasure, but there were enough riches for a man—and even his children's children!—to live in luxury for the rest of his days.

I descended the large central staircase down the main floor of the chamber. The only sound, which in the deathlike silence of the place seemed deafening, was the crackling of our flaming brands. Abd Al-Aziz followed cautiously, nervously glancing about. I picked up a scimitar with rubies set into the pommel and gave it a few swings. The blade was so well balanced it seemed like just an extension of my own arm. I decided that it would become a fine addition to my hall of trophies.

I walked about the chamber, lighting the sconces along the walls with my torch. At the far end of the chamber was a gigantic hole in the ground with a large candle-strewn altar built before it. The hole was perfectly circular, suggesting it was man-made. Where it led I couldn't begin to guess. I called back to Abd Al-Aziz, still peering into the gaping black void, imploring him to gather the most valuable items he could find for our packs.

The Libyan did not respond.

I turned back, wondering where he had gone. Again I called his name, and again there was no answer. I walked back to the center of the chamber, my scimitar held out before me. The immensity of the space around me was suddenly dizzying. I began breathing techniques I often used to steady myself when hunting big game out on the savannah. This helped to clear my mind and focus my thoughts.

It was then, after I had brought myself back from the verge of panic, that I saw my Libyan guide. He was standing not far from me, staring blankly at the altar atop which the candles suddenly burned brightly. His eyes were hazy and pale, like those of a blind man. I asked him what was wrong but he either ignored me or didn't hear, instead he walked slowly towards the ceremonial platform. I rested a hand on his shoulder as he passed. The Libyan finally looked at me as I did, though whether or not he actually saw me I can't be sure. Either way, he quickly resumed his unwavering march.

I nearly cried out as another form brushed past me. Then another, and another. I faltered, not knowing what to make of the spectacle I was witnessing—a spectacle no man should ever have to witness. I recognized most of them as the men in our entourage, or at least recognized the clothing they wore, as most of them sorely lacked the physical features of what had once made them human. They were little more than skeletons with shrunken skin stretched tight over her bones like dry seaweed. My legs froze, rooted to the spot despite every instinct screaming for me to run. There was little I could do as the desiccated dead filed in behind the Libyan towards the altar. Eventually I fell in line with the charnel procession—my legs hardly seeming to obey my commands—and came to stand just behind Abd Al-Aziz amongst the sepulchral congregation.

The Libyan held his hands up in supplication and chanted in a tongue unknown to me. The dead behind him remained chillingly silent. I hadn't noticed before, being too preoccupied with the mummified Arabs, but there was a shadowy, featureless human form bound to the altar. The shadow-man struggled against his ethereal bonds like a thing possessed. I watched in dread as the sacrificial rite unfolded before me.

The greater my unease became, the more the bound figure struggled.

A faint blue glow began to emanate from the cavernous pit as Abd Al-Aziz continued his mysterious chants. My heart was beating faster and faster, I knew I should have fled but was compelled to stay. By whatever merciful gods were watching the profane ritual, I should have fled! The ground beneath our feet began to rumble and shake, sending bits of debris raining down from above. The light grew stronger until I had to shield my eyes from the sheer intensity of it.

"*svāhā Apeptsut, asesha sakshi*," I heard the Libyan cry.

What I beheld then upon opening my eyes, while I still had eyes to witness such horror, would surely haunt me beyond the grave. The aberration that rose from the darkness of the pit was nothing that could have been contrived by nature. It opened wide its abysmal maw and glared down at me with eight shimmering cobalt eyes. The worm-like creature's hide was covered in a sort of gold plating that seemed to act as an exoskeleton, underneath which a strange bioluminescence shone through the gaps in its organic armor. I stared into that terrible maw for what seemed like eternity, shuddering at the thought of being torn to shreds on those cylindrical rows of jagged, inwardly facing teeth.

The mummified dead genuflected before the enormous monstrosity, as did Abd Al-Aziz. "*Apeptsut,*" he said reverently, bowing so low his forehead scraped the floor.

I gazed upon the abhorrent spectacle of this primeval god—what else could it have been?—and knew that I was gazing upon a being older than history. This creature had observed the rise and fall of empires; burrowed through primordial earth as continents drifted apart; dined on mammoths in the Cenozoic era and Mesozoic life millions of years before that.

In the same instant I lost my sight and my mental faculties were reduced to ruin. Just a fleeting glimpse of the deity was enough to shatter my mortal sensibilities and drive me into madness. For the briefest moment I experienced the uncanny sense of leaving my physical body. My transitory journey into the astrophysical ended when I again opened my eyes to find myself bound to an altar, Abd Al-Aziz beside me and the very maw of chaos hovering above. I struggled vainly against my bonds. Then I looked to the gathered dead and amongst their sallow faces saw my own hazy eyes, pale like a blind man's, scimitar still in hand. I understood then: the shadow-man was me — my soul.

The horror of that realization was the last conscious thought I had of that evil place, deep within the ancient ruins called *al-Maghrib* on accursed Cyrenaican sands. Now I float through perpetual darkness, caught in a surreal state of limbo. I imagine my physical body is now a mindless slave to Apeptsut and think that perhaps it was for the best that I was evicted from it.

My purgatory has revealed many things to me, perhaps because I have had infinite time to ponder them. I know now that our comprehension of the world we live in is simply a tenuous illusion, held together by our severely limited ability to process it. I shudder to think what would happen if we ever discovered the unimaginable horrors that lurked just beyond the veil of human perception! There are things hidden in the deepest recesses of the earth, where unhallowed ritual fires burn, that are far older and more malevolent than even Apeptsut.

Perhaps one day you too will see.

Ending Notes

Helsyndel spawned itself in my mind many years ago, nearly too many to count now. It started with just a sketch of the continent of Illthashore and grew with time. I began adding continents, which sprouted ideas, and that brought characters into existence and stories to fruition. I've much to learn yet about the writing craft, but many years later I was able to proudly produce what you have read here.

Helsyndel still has a long way to go before becoming a solidly fleshed out world, but each passing year it has grown exponentially—and it will continue to grow far into the future. Some content has not been added to this book, but that's only because I don't have a solid grasp on it yet. The next anthology will undoubtedly have new lands to explore, heinous villains to overcome, and heroes to save the day—or maybe the villains will save the day, who knows.

Regardless, I am merely a conduit for these lands, villains, and heroes to come to life via the written word. They exist in a far away place that can only be brought to life by imagination and the desire to make it real in my own mind and the mind of the reader.

For the many people who helped bring Helsyndel to these pages—especially my Granpda. who edited many of my stories—thank you.

May the adventure never cease

escapades. He will live on in the words that bring these adventures to life.

Printed in the USA
CPSIA information can be obtained
at www.ICGtesting.com
LVHW051636191223
766806LV00063B/1180